RVN Scout

L. R. LAVANCHER

Fulton Books, Inc.
Meadville, PA

Published by Fulton Books 2020

ISBN 978-1-64654-179-9 (paperback)
ISBN 978-1-64654-180-5 (digital)

Printed in the United States of America

CHAPTER 1

The Rock

As he looked out of the Flying Tiger aircraft window, he thought to himself how lucky a Sergeant in the Corps could get, more so in his first five years as a Marine. For his first assignment after A school, he was stationed as an Instructor/Inspector, MARTD, Marietta, Georgia a seventeen-year-old fresh from aviation ordnance school in Jacksonville, Florida. Then a change of MOS to Intelligence and school at Fort Holabird, Maryland, with hopes of assignment in early 1968 to Vietnam. The Corps had other plans and sent him back to the MARTD to replace the Staff Sergeant Intelligence Chief who got out because he didn't want to take the chance of going to war. The next two years, he was submitting an Administrative Action Form (AA) every ninety days and requesting reassignment to Vietnam. Perhaps it was a good thing because the time he spent at the MARTD provided the opportunity to hone his skills as an Intelligence Chief and learning the ins and outs as a Sergeant in the United States Marine Corps.

One of those skills he learned was giving a quart of Seagram's Seven to the Administrative Chief prior to the submission on the last AA to Headquarters Marine Corps the text "pending suitable replacement" conveniently omitted, and the orders to the staging battalion at Camp Pendleton soon arrived. So after two weeks' leave, he was at his Upstate New York home with friends and family, where they remarked how sharp and muscular his five-foot, nine-inch frame had become. Much of that had to do with humping 20 mm ammo cans up the spine of F-8 Crusaders as an Ordnance Man and a daily diet of Marine Corps physical fitness. Once again, Chesty, Dan

Daily, or whoever the guardian angel that was looking out for him shined. By late 1968, just after Christmas, he reported to staging.

No Officers and Staff Non-commissioned Officers, with the exception of a single SNCO, were checking in. It seemed M Company was comprised of only officers and staff noncommissioned officers, leaving N Company with a single Staff NCO and eight Sergeants in leadership positions. Based on the date of Rank, he found himself as Platoon Sergeant for the Second Platoon N Company at the Staging Battalion. The time spent at Pendleton was divided between training, medical exams, and of course, liberty, when his Platoon wasn't assigned duty. During this time, a strong bond was established with his fellow Sergeants and the Marines in his Platoon.

The Viet Cong Village taught Marines how to search a Village; while the John Wayne Course for immediate action as targets popped up while they patrolled a trail also, Booby Traps, both with and without explosives, plus land navigation for both day and night, to name a few. Finally, Mount Mother a huge hill climbed with full gear, were some of the N Company's training assignments.

Corpsmen checked over each member from head to toe and told of how salt tablets would be important. Every Marine dreaded the GG Shot short for gamma goblin, which felt like a square needle in the rear. Both Sergeants (Platoon Leader and Sergeant) enter Sick Bay and threw their shot cards on the table in front of the Corpsman who entered the GG on their cards and said, "Send in the Platoon single file shot cards in hand."

Both Sergeants looked at each other in the eyes and spoke almost simultaneously, "I'm not getting one if you aren't!"

After the Platoon finished with their shots, the Corpsman had suggested running a mile or so to loosen the muscle on the buttocks and get the GG into their system. He almost felt guilty by not getting one but thought, *Rank has its privileges*, as he double-timed the Platoon down the road.

Some of the liberty highlights first as a Platoon, the Orange River was endangered of flooding its banks and the civilians requested the Marine Corps help. He was very proud of 2nd Platoon when 2 to the man volunteered to help. Dropped off at a location along side the raging river close to a huge pile of sand, sandbags and shovels the Marines began to work.

Looking around He noticed the trucks which transported them were absent as well as anyone with any authority. Noon chow approached and the Platoon Sergeant inquired do you have any food for His men. Of course, Murphy's Law fell upon the Unit when the answer was No. A hat was passed among the Platoon.

"I'll be back with some chow. George, come with me."

Private George was a fellow New Yorker and Sergeant Latoure's runner, house mouse and any other duty that might arise tagged along side.

A Safeway grocery store was only three blocks away, and off the pair went to get some chow for the Platoon. George's first task was to count the slices of bread in a loaf and divide it by two. Then he threw enough loaves to feed the unit two sandwiches each. Latoure went and grabbed baloney, cheese, mustard, mayonnaise, and lettuce. Large bottles of soda, paper cups, and potato chips finished off the shopping. Ten dollars of Latoure's money plus the Platoon's donations covered the total bill. He told the clerk they were "borrowing" the two carts to bring the food to the Platoon.

Smiling, she said, "Fine."

And off they went. Maybe it was because the Marines were starving or whatever the reason, one and all said it was the best meal they had in a very long time.

"Hustle the carts back to the store, George."

"Aye, aye," George replied as he headed out.

Some more highlights of the time at Camp Pendleton included George again. Most of the Platoon went on the Liberty Bus for a weekend around Disneyland. Sergeants Latoure and Gleason, an air delivery Marine, shared the bill for a room at the Caravan Motel, which was almost directly across the street from Disney. Walking the streets, the closest lounge was open at noon, so the two entered for cocktails. The bartender was very nice and cute as well. She told them to come back at eight that evening if they had coats and ties to wear because it was ladies' night. Of course, neither had any, so planning began for an alternate evening as they returned to the room.

As luck would have it, before getting to the motel, Latoure noticed George strolling across the street; and in a command voice, "George!"

In an instant, he was in front of the two Sergeants. "I have a task for you to see if you can handle it, Private George. Sergeant Gleason and I have been invited to a party, but it requires coat and tie. See what you can come up with."

George smiled and took off.

Latoure shouted, "Room 222, right here!"

"What are the chances that will happen?" Gleason asked.

"Who knows, but we should pick up some booze at that liquor store across the street just in case," said Latoure.

Champagne was on sale, so they bought three bottles and put them on ice back at the room. It was time for a power nap, as they both crashed.

Both were startled from their nap with a pounding on the room's door.

"It's me," George spoke before either could ask who was there. George stood in the doorway with two American Airlines blazers with ties hanging from the pockets. With an ear-to-ear grin, George asked, "Will this work? I have to return them by 10:00 a.m. tomorrow."

"Sure will," Gleason said.

He had picked up one of the champagne bottles and handed it to George. "Speak to no one about this either," Latoure added. "And Semper Fi!"

They made up a story. One would be the engineer (Gleason) because of his air delivery background, the other the navigator (Latoure) because of his intelligence background. Their haircuts were because they were Marine Reserves.

To say it worked would be an understatement at best. The champagne was put to good use, both as a drink and a lotion to massage two lovely ladies who spent the night with them. Around nine thirty, the knock on the door woke up all four. George was there to pick up the blazers. On tiptoes, he was trying to see who was in the room with the two Sergeants, but to no avail.

"Thanks, George, I won't forget this." As the door closed in George's face. It will be a Washington's Birthday he will always remember.

The final Camp Pendleton memory was the steak dinner the eight Sergeants shared at Marty's Valley Inn, outside the rear gate. One and all thought it would be awhile before steaks would be eaten during their tours in Vietnam. Each ordered the T-bone steak dinner for two—a two-pound porterhouse with all the fixings. The waitress seemed concerned, but each consumed the entire meal, or rather inhaled it. Latoure always thought it was the equivalent of a last supper, se only God knew which one of those Sergeants would be retu' ne. On March of 1969, training was completed, and all ha Vietnam; the only negative was his orders read First Marir Wing, Republic of Vietnam.

N Company boarded the aircraft with destination as Kadena Air Force Base, Okinawa. It was an uneventful flight, to say the least, as the plane set down on The Rock. Currently, Okinawa was still under US control, so both the money and laws were based on familiar rules and regulations. Upon deplaning, there were three gray navy buses waiting on the tarmac. According to rank, Officers the Staff NCOs got off. Next were seven of the eight Sergeants of N Company; one had gotten the creepy crud in Oceanside and was on medical hold, along with a dozen or so troops. The Sergeants took up the front of the second bus, while the remaining Marines and corpsmen piled on both the second and the last bus.

It was only a short drive down the road to Camp Butler or Camp Foster depending on which Gate you entered. Sergeants headed straight into the Headquarters Building which looked like a converted barracks orders in hand. Upon entering the S-1 (Administration), there were 4 desks all with Admin Clerks at the ready to process the new arrivals. Once again, his guardian smiled down on him. He mentioned to the clerk that orders to either First or Third Division would have been better; at least he was headed to the Dance.

Corporal Jones looked up and spoke, "I can fix that, but you will have to spend about a week here on "Oki" while you wait for the next Grunt Tiger flight. And of course, buy me a few drinks in the "Ville" for what I am going to do for you." A concerned look washed over Latoure's face as the Admin Clerk reach for a huge rubber stamp.

In less than a second, the stamp made a resounding thud and then revealed "FIRST MARINE DIVISION." The Corporal gave directions to the NCO quarters and said, "Get squared away. I will look you up after 1630."

Just like that, his orders were amended, and within a week's time, he was joining the First Marine Division in the Republic of Vietnam.

How fortunate could anyone be, Latoure thought as he checked in with the duty. "Corporal Jones called and let me know you would be staying on the Rock for a week or so. That being the case, you can have the room on the left leading into the squad bay. The only thing you need from your seabag is a set of Charlies because for sure you will have Duty NCO at least once while you are here. Tomorrow you will get your issue for use in-country. By the way, give your uniform to the *mama-san*. She is floating around here someplace to square your Charlies away for only a pack of smokes." The Duty NCO informed Latoure.

"Thanks and Semper Fi. Tell Corporal Jones where you put me up." He spent the better part of the next two 2 hours digging out his Charlies, making his rack, hunting down Mama-san, and hitting the rain room. Even with all that it was only 1400 so He took out a set of satins better known as the Utility uniform. Both uniforms made the trip in decent shape; a little buffing and the boots returned to their high shine, and a quick press with an iron to smooth out the creases in the utilities. He glanced at his watch. It was 1430; two more hours before Jones showed up, so off to the Marine Corps Exchange he went, following the directions of the duty.

Okinawa in March was like spring in the States, with temperatures in the midseventies and a bright sunshine. Thinking ahead like a good NCO, Latoure purchased civilian shirt and trousers. Adding a carton of Marlboros and some toiletries, shopping was completed. A soda from the slop chute helped to use up some time as he took in the local scenery. Dozens of women—military, civilian, and local—passed by his table. *This place is awesome,* he thought to himself.

Upon returning to the barracks, the First Sergeant was there and asked, "Friday or Saturday, which one you want to stand Sergeant of the Guard?"

"Either is fine with me, First Sergeant," Latoure answered.

"Okay then, Friday night you have the duty."

"Aye, Aye!" was his reply, and he headed toward the room. Mama-san was in the room hanging up the Charlies, and boy, they look super. With a smile, he handed her not one but two packs of Marlboros.

She started pointing at his utilities and saying in broken English, "I do, I do."

At that time, his Japanese was very limited, but he did recall *domo* meant "thanks" and told her the same. Friday was still three days away, so no problem that she would have them ready by then.

There was still forty-five minutes before Jones was due to show up, so lying down on top of the rack for a power nap was in order. The nap was abruptly interrupted—which seemed like five minutes later, but it was over an hour—with a pounding on the hatch.

True to his word, Jones was there and said, "Come on, sleepyhead. Let's get some chow."

As He passed the duty NCO, he handed a liberty card, which really wasn't needed by Sergeants, but going with the flow, he stuck it in his wallet. Both were wearing civilian clothes, anticipating a night on the town. Chow was decent, as many mama-sans moved throughout the chow hall, picking up dishes and trash.

Looking at Jones, he said, "Pretty neat setup you have here, Jones. First Shirt told me I have the duty Friday, so what other things will I have to accomplish before then?"

Jones replied, "Other than getting your issue from supply, nothing but enjoying the Rock. So tonight, we will take in some nightlife and maybe a steam and cream."

"What the heck is that?" Latoure asked.

"You'll see," Jones replied, laughing. "Let's stop by the club first, okay?"

"Sure, sounds great," he answered.

The NCO club was on the first floor of a barracks. Slot machines lined the walls; nickels, dimes, and quarters were in the room just off the entrance, as they entered the club. Nice-looking local girls were waiting tables and hustling drinks.

After getting their first drink, Jones asked, "Want to try the slots?"

"Why not." Latoure had a pocketful of coins and a few singles from his Exchange visit earlier, so denomination by denomination, he worked his way through the slots. Nickels and dimes were donated, but when the first quarter was played, three bells appeared. *Eighteen quarters. Not bad,* he thought.

"Yes!" Jones yelled. Looking over his shoulder, Latoure saw two watermelons and a bar on Jones's quarter machine.

"Looks like you are buying tonight, Jones," he announced. Not paying attention and talking over his shoulder, he asked, "How much you win?" Before Jones could answer, Latoure's quarter machine flashed as three watermelons stopped on the pay line.

"Well, that's $18.75 apiece, so it's time to hit the Village," Jones replied.

"So what will it be? Kitamae just outside the gate or a taxi downtown to the real nightlife? How far will our winnings take us, Jones?"

"If you have another ten or twenty to go with it, a long way!" Jones said.

"Let's stay local tonight, and Saturday, we can check out downtown, okay?" Latoure's said.

They started walking to the Foster gate, which was only a couple hundred yards from the NCO club, which led to the Village of Zukeran.

Standing outside the Foster gate, looking across Okinawa Highway 58, the Village was lighted by a myriad of neon lights, which offered all sorts of delights. Restaurants, lounges, and massages; you name it, and most likely you could find it in Zukeran. As they waited for the light to turn green, Jones went over some of the good things and the scams they would encounter that evening. With the light turning green, it was off to new adventures for Latoure. Jones informed him that the Club Zukeran, with its restaurant on the second floor, was the most popular with the Marines. He, however, liked the Club Misty at the far end of the block. It was friendlier, and the girls were good for their word and hardly ever tried to scam a Marine; that is, unless he had it coming for being an idiot.

Jones was very popular at the Club Misty, and many of the girls bade him good evening with broad smiles on their faces. He introduced Latoure to them and moved toward a booth at the rear of the club. A girl sat by Jones, and he introduced her as Midori-san, his number one girl. Smiling, she slapped Jones on the thigh then began to wave to another girl to come sit. Latoure noticed her palm was facing down as she gestured for a girl named Michiko-san.

As she approached, she asked Latoure, "Dijobu disuka?"

Jones told Latoure, "She is asking if it is okay to sit by you."

"How would I answer in Japanese?" Latoure inquired.

"Hi so disu," Jones told him, which Latoure smiled and told Michiko, trying to copy Jones.

You could order by the glass or the bottle, of which the selection was limited. Seagram's Seven, Chivas Regal scotch, or Suntory, a Japanese whiskey. Jones told him that buying a bottle was a lot cheaper but because Latoure was leaving the Rock soon, by the glass would be better.

"Give me ten bucks, and we will drink from my bottle, okay?"

"Sound great." was the reply.

The two girls drank from the same bottle and mixed the Seagram's Seven with water. Jones explained that if a girl asked to buy her a drink, not only would it cost five bucks, but more than likely, it was fruit juice. Latoure thought to himself that Jones was an excellent authority on liberty on Okinawa.

During the course of the evening, Jones, as well as the two girls speaking in passable English, talked about anything and everything about their home. From English being taught in school to the use of US currency and driving on the right-hand side of the road. It was almost like being in the States, apart from most of the signs being in both languages, plus the girls' accent. After less than twenty-four hours on the Rock, he had to admit to himself Okinawa wasn't as bad as scuttlebutt had led one to believe.

It was well after 1:00 a.m. when Jones asked if he was hungry or if Latoure wanted to call it a night. With both the date and time change, he was getting hungry and told Jones so.

"You don't mind if the girls come with us, do you?"

So all four stood up; Jones and the girls spoke to the Mama-san behind, which he did not hear completely nor understand. They took a right turn out of the Club Misty and walked by all the clubs, which were still active with music and laughter. Just past the Zukeran Club was a very steep set of stairs where the girls and Jones started up.

The Zukeran Restaurant was very busy with mostly Marines and a few Sailors sitting at tables. Two waitresses were hustling plates of food, carrying four, five, or six plates at a time. A jukebox was belting out popular songs of the time. Midori said something to one of the waitstaff, and it didn't sound like Japanese to Latoure. Jones explained to him that the Okinawan language was called *Hogan*, and he only knew how to say thank-you. Midori must have asked if taking the table in the far corner was okay because that was where they sat. Menus were in both English and kanji, so it didn't present any problem deciding what to eat. Jones ordered beef and peppers while the girls, soba. Latoure thought he heard "yakisoba." Beef and peppers sounded good to Latoure, so orders were placed with coffee for all. Both his meal and the coffee were great. He asked the girls what it was that they were eating, and Latoure had heard correctly; "yakisoba" was the answer. It resembled spaghetti noodles with a mixture of different vegetables and looked very tasty to him.

All throughout the evening, both at the club and now while they ate, he often caught Michiko staring at him. It didn't make Latoure uncomfortable in the least, but he wondered what she was thinking.

She looked at Midori and said, "Robert De Niro."

Midori shook her head and replied, "Paul Newman, dis su!"

Jones laughed out loud. "They are trying to decide which movie star you look like the most."

Latoure smiled and recalled the same conversation happened back in the States between the two Girls he and Gleason dated that Holiday evening.

"I am not going back to base, Midori and I, rather she has a small apartment just around back here."

Latoure looked at Michiko, who turned a deep shade of red. "Dijobu, Michiko-san?"

"Joto!" she answered.

Not being familiar with Okinawa or Zukeran for that matter, Latoure said, "I best be heading back to the barracks. I don't want Michiko thinking I am a dirty old man!" Turning toward Michiko, he spoke, "But I would like to see you again this Saturday evening if you are going to be working at Club Misty?"

She resembled a bobblehead doll as fast as her head was moving up and down. "Okay, eight o'clock. I will see you there."

"Michiko lives in the same building as Midori, so I will escort her home, Sarge."

"Thanks and Semper Fi, Jonesy!"

They pooled their money and left a nice tip for the waitress who ensured their coffee cups never got empty.

The steps were so steep they reminded him of Mount Mother at Camp Pendleton; however, going down was a lot easier. He hugged both girls and once again thanked Jones. The crosswalk was almost directly in front of the door; Latoure walked straight, and Jones with both girls turned right and right again, walking down an alley. He flashed his Military ID at the Gate Sentry who waved him through. About three hundred yards later, he was at the barracks, then a quick change and an even quicker shower, it was sack time. Latoure looked at the clock, it was 3:00 a.m.; he set the alarm for 7:00 a.m. and crashed like a lead balloon.

It felt like he just closed his eyes when the alarm began ringing. Up and at 'em! Time for the three S's: shit, shower, and shave. Then he put on the fresh set of utilities Mama-san had laid out for him. The lap of luxury and duty on Okinawa was a very decent place. He was walking out of the barracks as the formation was forming, and using a little brain power, he figured the last Platoon was the fourth duty section.

He walked up to the Sergeant standing in the Platoon Sergeant's position and stated, "July '67."

The Sergeant nodded and took up the Right Guide's Position after informing Latoure, "All Present and Accounted for!" A quick shuffling of the ranks, and all was ready for the Company formation.

"Attention!" the First Sergeant commanded as he took the position in front of the Company.

The command was echoed by the 4 Platoon Sergeants. The First Sergeant made an about-face as the Company Commander approached.

"Sir, the Company is formed."

"Post" was the Company Commander's order, followed by "Report" as the First Sergeant took up his position to the left of the Company Commander.

In turn, all 4 Platoon Sergeants saluted and reported, "All present and accounted for."

"Very well, carry out the Plan of the Day. Dismissed."

"Aye, Aye, Sir!" the Platoon Sergeants replied in unison.

Just that quickly, the formation was over.

Latoure hunted down Jones, who was looking for Him at the same time. Jones spoke, "You made a nice impression on the girls last night. They want the 4 of Us to do something together this weekend."

"Which day, Saturday or Sunday?" Latoure asked.

"Both" was Jones's reply.

"Sounds great. Where's Supply, Corporal Jones?" Jones pointed down the road at another old barracks.

"It's the one with the 2 ash cans flanking the entrance. I will catch up with you for noon chow. By the way. Disbursing is 2 more buildings down from Supply, if you need cash or need to square away your finances."

"Thanks, Corporal Jones. I'll swing by Admin around 11:30 for chow." Jones nodded as they went their separate ways.

Latoure took his time heading for supply to give the Marines a chance to move from the formation to their appointed place of duty.

So, after saluting colors sharply at 0800, up the ladder to Supply, he went. Marines use nautical terms like their brothers in the Navy. For example, ladder/stairs; hatch/door; bulkhead/wall.

"What can I do for you, Sarge?" The Supply Clerk asked.

"Well, I just arrived yesterday with a short pause before heading out to Viet Nam. Corporal Jones is working up the change to my orders."

"Give me a few minutes, and I will put your issue together. Fill out the top of the card, please, while I do." The Supply Cerk had been doing this for a really long time, so he knew just by looking what sizes Latoure wore except for the boots.

Size 9 1/2 before he even had a chance to ask.

Latoure's issue began to pile up on the counter as he looked at it for serviceability. It really wasn't necessary as it all was brand-new gear.

"Jones told me you were a decent guy and I should fix you up right. So how about a B-4 Bag to put this all in, Sergeant Latoure?"

Latoure smiled there was that Guardian Angel again. "Thanks, I owe you a beer, Corporal."

"Here's a set of stencils use this marker to put your last name on that white rectangle on the side."

Latoure slid the metal stencils together, spelling out his last name, then stenciled the B-4 bag as the Clerk finished getting his issue together. The Corporal filled out the supply card item by item for Latoure's gear as he watched.

"That's it you are all set. I will be at the Club for that beer tonight."

"I will see you there. Can I set this issue to the side while I take a quick trip to Disbursing? You look like you can pound down some beer. I had better get some more money."

Laughing out loud, the Clerk said, "No problem, Sergeant Latoure. I will set it at the end of the counter for you."

"Semper Fi!" Latoure spoke, heading out the hatch.

Latoure had missed a payday with his travels from Staging to Okinawa. His base pay was around $343 a month, so half of that was due. At that time, military was receiving checks on the 15th and 30th of each month. As soon as He arrived in Viet Nam, the $95 combat/ overseas pay would begin.

"Let me have $150 and put the rest on the books please," Latoure informed the Pay clerk.

"Can Do," the reply. The Disbursing Officer came to the counter, checked Latoure's ID, and gave him $150.

"Thank you, Sir." As Latoure left to pick up his supply issue.

"I am grabbing my gear, Corporal!" Latoure yelled to the Supply Clerk, who was busy at the rear of Supply.

"Okay, no problem, see you around 1800 at the Club, Sergeant Latoure."

"I will bring Corporal Jones with me as well."

"Sounds great. OohRah!"

It was almost like a seabag drag, lugging that B-4 bag back to the barracks. Mama-san had dollar signs in her eyes as she watched Latoure carry the bag into his room.

"Wait until I call you, Mama-san, *dozo*."

"Hai," she replied.

He went over the supply card, making sure nothing was missing while he took that short trip to disbursing. It was all there as he suspected it would be. He called Mama-san, and when she came into his room, he gave her a set of jungle utilities to press for him and asked if she had any shoe polish. She shook her head wildly as she always does when asked a question and spoke, "I do, I do!"

"No, Mama-san, I do boots. You do uniform. *Joto desu ka.*"

"Hai!" was her reply and hustled out to get the polish for Latoure.

It was only 0930. Latoure had plenty of time to put down a good base on his boots. Some might say, "Why bother starching or pressing jungle utilities and spit shining boots?"

To them, Latoure would say, "You don't get a second chance to make a first impression." It had served him well so far in his five-plus years as a Marine. He stopped shining his boots around 1115, cleaned up, and headed out to meet with Corporal Jones.

Jones acknowledge Latoure's presence with a nod of his head while holding up a single finger, meaning it would be just a minute.

Work being accomplished, Jones walked up to Latoure and said, "I am starving!"

"The corporal from supply will be joining us tonight at the club, if not for chow," Latoure said.

"That's Corporal Denny. Pretty cool dude if you ask me."

"Well, thanks to you, he really hooked me up in supply, so I owe him a beer or two."

"What he do for you?"

"Issued me a B-4 bag for starters, plus brand-new jungles, boots, and web gear."

On the way to the chow hall, Jones told him that he hardly got any sleep last night, not because he and Midori were doing the wild thing but because Michiko and Midori wouldn't stop discussing Latoure.

"What was said, Jonesy?"

"Heck, my Japanese is decent but not that good, so here is the translation, according to Midori. Michiko said you were very handsome, and you respected her honor by not trying to touch or do anything to make her uncomfortable. You knew they were trying to decide De Niro or Newman, right?" Latoure laughed hard. Then Jones continued, "In case you didn't know, Midori and I are together, and Michiko is her cousin. That means Midori has to approve of who Michiko dates, and you, my friend, won the brass ring." They arrived at the chow hall as Jones finished up by saying, "We can work out details tonight at the club, okay?"

"Sure thing, Jonesy."

Once again, the food was excellent; full salad bar, fried chicken, mashed potatoes with gravy, who could ask for more? Corporal Denny wasn't more than two or three minutes behind them, and Sergeant Latoure motioned to him to join their table. Most of the conversation was where their duty stations were and how Latoure got so lucky to receive I & I orders right out of A school. Both received orders to Marine Corps Base at Camp Butler straight from Staging Battalion, instead of Vietnam. They were kind of disappoint not going to Vietnam, but Latoure thought it was lucky for him they did not. Plans to meet at the club around 1800, where the drinks would be on Sergeant Latoure, were set.

Latoure decided to swing by the Exchange on his way back from chow to pick up something else to wear besides the clothes he purchased yesterday. He did not feel the need for a lot of civilian clothes, just a couple of shirts and another pair of trousers. Mama-san was on his mind as he threw into the basket another carton of smokes. He thought about the girls and picked up two like trinkets that cost him two dollars apiece.

Back at the barracks, he began putting a high shine on both his jungle boots and then his dress shoes. Mama-san brought his jungles into the room and hung them in the wall locker.

"Mama-san, take this carton of cigarettes and let me know what more you need for all the help you have given me."

"This okay. No more. You number one!" she replied.

He did an inventory of all the gear to make sure he was ready for duty NCO and all the liberty Jones had planned. When finished, he had another power nap to make up for the lack of sleep last evening.

His obligation to both corporals paid with a couple of pitchers of beer, handshakes, and oorahs, he and Jones headed toward Zukeran and the Club Misty. After a shallow bow followed by beautiful smiles, the girls led the two Marines back to the table at the rear of the club. Latoure had given one of the two small boxes he had bought at the Exchange. Inside was a costume jewelry depicting a butterfly with jewels in the wings. Little did either of the Marines knew, but butterflies represented someone who ran around with many rather than a few. Latoure bought them because he thought they were pretty. It took some convincing, but finally the two girls forgave Latoure as he passed the gift. A few tense moments passed between Midori and Jones as she said something to Jones, asking if he thought she ran around on him.

Jones, in true fashion, passed the buck to Latoure and said, "He bought!"

Latoure tried to defuse the situation by offering. "I bought them because I thought they were as beautiful as you two girls are."

The girls looked at one another and back at the Marines saying, "Dijobu, domo arigato."

Latoure also gave Midori twenty dollars to buy another bottle of Seagram's. "Put Jones's name, *dozo*, Midori-san."

The rest of the evening passed without any further incident. Latoure took every chance he could to take long and loving looks at Michiko. He felt that pushing himself on her was not in the best interest, so he played it cool, as the saying goes. There was a lot of laughter, smiles, and eye-to-eye contact between Michiko and Latoure. On the other hand, along with the smiles and laughter, Jones was punched more than once on the arm for things he said or perhaps did. Jones also explained that neither he nor Latoure would be able to come to the club because of Marine Corps duties over the next couple of days. The girls looked disappointed, but Jones softened the blow by saying he was going to rent a car for Saturday and Sunday for the four of them.

They began nodding their heads very rapidly and saying, "Hai, hai, hai!" Hugs were shared, and the Marines left to return to Camp Foster.

Latoure didn't know, but Headquarter and Service Company schedule a Physical Fitness Test for Permanent Personnel. Latoure was Transit, so he did not need to take the test, but he would be required to be a monitor for the test. Latoure wished Jones had given him a heads-up, but monitoring the PFT, as it was referred to, would help pass his time on the Rock. Both Denny and Jones scored first class on the test; one step closer to those elusive Sergeant's stripes for both.

Latoure thought Jones would like to stay on the Rock for his entire service in the Corps if Midori would have him.

Latoure spent the rest of that day and the following exploring both Camp Butler and Camp Foster, as well as the Villages outside all four gates. Throughout his travels, he learned the Club Cherry outside the East Gate of Foster in the Village of Chatan is where all the Intel Types hung out. The Camp Butler northern gate led to the busy Okinawa City District with a myriad of different shops and restaurants. He had never tried sushi, so at one of the small cafés type, he gave Maguro, a red tuna, in a seaweed wrap a try. He wasn't prepared for the hot wasabi that was inside which curled his toenails. The remaining of the week, he had lunch or evening chow with either Denny or Jones the rest of the week, and before he knew it, Friday was there; and at 0745, he reported in as the H & S duty NCO for Camp Foster, Okinawa, Japan.

After checking out both the duty roster plus the rules and regulations for his role as duty NCO, he began reading the logbook entries for the previous weekend as placed by his predecessors. Other than a few men who were drunk and disorderly, not much else happened. There were no inbound flights from either Vietnam or the States until Monday, so he didn't have to concern himself with any new arrivals. Both Denny and Jones stopped by the duty desk to see how things were going. Jones was going out to Club Misty and planned on spending the night with Midori, if she would have him. He asked to tell Michiko he thought about her and was looking forward to seeing her again.

The officer of the day (OOD) stopped by around 1800 just to see how things were going and told Latoure he would be back for evening colors. Uneventful would be the word Latoure used to describe his twenty-four hours as the H & S duty NCO. He had to snatch a knot in a couple of Marines fighting in the barracks and threw one in a cold shower, clothes and all. He was relieved promptly at 0745 by another Sergeant he had never seen before. The few minutes the two talked, Latoure learn that the new Sergeant was also waiting on a flight to Vietnam.

His assistant duty NCO had relieved him during the course of the evening, so Latoure did get a few hours of sleep. He had just finished with his three S's and was getting dressed when Jones showed up, knocking at his door. He had already given Jones money for his part of the car rental, so Jones told him there were no Cadillacs left, so he had to get a pedal-powered vehicle. Of course, Jones was joking.

"What's on the agenda for the day?" Latoure asked.

"The girls have it all planned out. I guess we will know when we pick them up at 0900." Jones replied then added, "Grab your shaving kit and change of clothes, at least clean skivvies, I'll put them in my ditty bag. You won't be coming back here until Sunday evening."

All loaded up, Jones drove out of the Camp Foster gate, heading south on Okinawa 58, and took the first right-hand turn and then another right almost immediately. He pulled up alongside an apartment-style building where both got out and headed up the stairs to the second floor. Jones knocked on the second apartment door, which swung open very quickly. Latoure saw arms go around Jones's neck as both began trying to squeeze the breath out of each other. Michiko peeked around the two lovers and, as usual, did her shallow bow like she always did. Her eye contact with his eyes seemed to search his soul.

Jones reached just inside the apartment door and picked up a small piece of luggage. When the girls stepped into the walkway, Latoure was awestruck. Both girls were wearing slacks with flared legs and colorful button-down shirts—the style in 1969. To say they were a vision of beauty would have been an understatement. They went down the stairs to the car rental, where Jones opened the trunk as Latoure opened both passenger side doors. With his palm, he motioned Midori to the front and Michiko to the rear seats. He slid in the passenger side as Michiko moved over to give him room. He could talk to Jones as well as look and even chat with Michiko.

Backtracking the way they came in, Jones then turned right on Okinawa 58, heading toward Naha. Of course, no one would let Latoure know where they were going until Jones made a left on Okinawa 82. He saw the road signs, noting that they were headed toward Shuri Castle, the former capital of the Ryukyu Kingdom built in the 1300s. To the Marines, it had a different meaning as it was the final defense line of the Japanese for the Battle of Okinawa. From April 1, 1945, and for the next eighty-two days, it marked the last and most costly engagement of World War II. He noticed another sign which read ten miles to Shuri Castle and an arrow pointing in the direction. Jones turned right just after the sign and pulled up to a building which looked like a very small hotel.

In English, there was the name Minshuku Getto. Jones went and opened the trunk, and both Marines picked up all the luggage.

Jones told Latoure that *minshuku* was like a bed and breakfast in the States, and the prices were more like half of what a hotel room in Naha would have cost them. Jones tried in almost passable Japanese to get two adjoining rooms; with Midori's assistance, the rooms were paid for, and the four walked up the stairs to the second floor. As they walked down the hall, they were wearing the sandals provided because they were required to leave their shoes at the entrance, which Midori placed in a small locker for them. It reminded Latoure of photographs of ancient Japanese homes with doorframes covered in white rice paper.

Halfway down the walkway, Jones and Midori stopped and pointed to the next set of sliding doors. They slid open the door to what was going to be their room, and Michiko grabbed his arm and basically dragged him down the hall to the next set of doors. She slid open the doors and who was standing in the room but Jones and Midori, laughing out loud. There were similar doors adjoining the rooms. The floors were bamboo tatami mats, each one meter long by half meter wide. Closets aligned the opposite wall, which Midori opened, revealing futon bedding and pillows.

She said, "Michiko will put your beds together this evening. Don't worry, GI."

She had a devilish grin on her face as she spoke. Jones showed Latoure a long stick, about two inches square, and said, "This is the door lock, Sergeant Latoure. You place it in the track, which prevents the door from being slid open."

"Listen, Jonesy, you can call me Larry while we are out and about, but return to the proper military address when we return," Latoure told Jones.

He answered, "Will do, Sarge!"

Latoure was no saint by any stretch of the imagination. The champagne massage in California was testament to that. He felt that spending the evening with Michiko was taking advantage of her, knowing that he was off to Vietnam sometime in the near future. He thought she was something special and a very beautiful woman to boot. She must have been reading his mind because when he looked in her direction, their eyes met. This time, she didn't look away or down as she had in the past.

"Ikima sho." Translation: "Let's go." Midori said this, ending the silence.

"Better grab our windbreakers. It might be a little windy at Shuri," Jones said.

With their shoes recovered and car loaded, off they went farther out Okinawa 82. In less than fifteen minutes, they pulled into the parking area of Shuri Castle.

Shuri Castle rests on over 47,160 square kilometers. They strolled over stone walkways and up stone stairs guarded by tall walls also of stone; each led to over twelve different destinations. Each one in its own right told stories of the castle. The grounds were impeccably kept, as flora showed throughout. At the top of the four-hundred-meter hill sat Shuri Castle, offering views of the South China Sea to the west and the Pacific Ocean to the east. He was looking left and right, standing outside the entrance.

"Ornate" would be the word Latoure used in describing his thoughts about Shuri Castle. He imagined the effort it took to return the castle after it had been totally destroyed during the Battle for Okinawa.

Midori explained to them that in restoring the castle, only traditional tools were used; meaning no power tools or modern technology. There were three separate courts, but only the last was for the king of the Ryukyus. Walking the grounds took them over three hours, so lunch seemed to be on everyone's mind. After a ten-minute walk, and they were headed back toward Naha. Shortly after leaving Shuri, they decided to stop at a small restaurant within ten minutes of the castle.

"Don't eat too much," the girls warned the two Marines. "We are going out to eat at a number one restaurant and club this evening."

The menus were in kanji rather than English, so Midori gave a quick description of what was offered while pointing to a wax likeness in a display case at the entrance. *Tonkatsu*, as she described it, looked very similar to a veal cutlet, so that was Latoure's choice. Service was fast; and the food looked delicious and tasted even better; that was how he would describe the lunch.

As the final few kilometers went by, the two women were in a lengthy conversation. Latoure caught the words *irikomiyu* and *akakaki*. Jones was just as much in the dark as Latoure. Shoes were changed, then they went up the stairway to their rooms.

Midori pointed to the end of the hallway and said, "Inkomiyu!"

The Marines understood half of the conversation, but *akakaki* still eluded them. Upon entering Latoure and Michiko's room, she walked to the closet and took out two robes, not terry cloth but cotton. She handed him one while speaking in a very shy voice.

"You change, nothing on, naked, *dozo*." He turned his back to her and did as she asked; unknown to him that she was doing almost the very same thing.

The door between the rooms started to rattle; Michiko had placed a long stick in the trough to prevent access, without asking. Latoure picked up the stick as the door began to slide open.

Jones spoke, "We are in for a treat, buddy!" Both were dressed the same, and they went out the door, down the hall, to the public bath.

The very size was amazing; there was a tiled area in the front, which had small stools similar to milking stools, but the legs were only six inches tall. In the rear was a huge bath, perhaps twice the size of any jacuzzi he had seen in the States. Steam rose from the bath like a morning mist. The girls ushered them toward the stools while taking off the Marines' robes, hanging them on pegs along the wall. It was kind of uncomfortable standing nude next to Jones, but Midori said in a voice that would make a drill instructor proud, "Sit!" *Akakaki* was the term used to describe the women who washed people in the baths.

In the next five or ten minutes, both of them were in someplace other than earth. The women, using huge natural sponges, first wet the Marines' bodies, then repeated with soap, scrubbing every square inch. This was the first intimate contact with Michiko he had, which took all his will power not to become too excited. She scrubbed then rinsed him with a dishpan-like thing three times. Latoure heard a slap on the butt as Midori told Jones, "Tub and no peeking, GI."

They wanted us to go in that huge tub and face the bulkhead. They would join us after they washed. Around five minutes later, she said, "Go to other side. No peeking until I say."

Midori definitely was in charge of this operation. Latoure laughed inside, knowing better not to do it out loud. "Dijobu!" she said, both then turned, facing the women.

The girls had joined them in the bath, floating shoulder deep in the very hot water, which barely distorted their nudity. Midori slowly moved toward Jones and shoved Latoure's back, pushing him toward Michiko. Their eyes once again locked as he approached.

"*Domo* for the bath, Michiko-san!" She just smiled in return. She was struggling because of her height and looked like a fishing bobber, moving up and down. Latoure took her hand and pulled her closer so she could rest on his knee, facing sideways, away from Jones and Midori. He lost track of time and was awoken from his trance created by the closeness and softness of Michiko's bare skin against his body.

"Time to get some rest before we head out tonight, Sarge."

What happened next kind of shocked Latoure; both women stood up and began walking to get their robes. Both girls' hair fell down their backs to the top of their buttocks. When in Rome; the Marines followed closely behind. It was a short trip through the hallway to the rooms, and this time, Latoure placed the stick in the trough and heard the echo from the other side of the door. *Great minds think alike, Jones,* he thought to himself.

While he was locking the door, so to speak, Michiko was busy laying out the futon bedding and pillows. Both were still wearing the robes from the pool, so after the bedding was ready, she nonchalantly removed her robe then slid under the futon, patting her hand at the futon on her left. He didn't need a second invitation; in less than a second, he was lying beside her. He put his arm under her neck; she understood, as she lifted her head while moving closer, placing it on his chest, and her nude body was melting into his. Latoure sensed that Michiko was nervous, so rather than make her anymore uncomfortable, he kissed her tenderly then laid back. Totally relaxed from the bath, sleep was soon upon them both.

Latoure felt Michiko's hand tapping then shaking his right shoulder. He turned and looked into those sparkling almond eyes.

"We go soon!" she said.

Both turned their backs to each other. He laughed inside. *Which one of us was shier?*

The door rattled, and he heard Jones say, "I've got a shirt and tie for you to wear. You will need it where we are going."

Latoure slid it open and was handed the shirt and tie. At the same time, Michiko left the room and headed toward the bathroom with Midori. He was looking back at Jones, in time to hear "We are going to a jazz club called Green Ants, plus eating at a top-notch restaurant."

"Sounds good. I slept like a baby. That bath was great."

Surprisingly, the girls did not take that long getting ready to go. Each wore a midthigh miniskirt, Ivy League shirt with button-down collars, and stylish shoes. Makeup was used very sparingly; however, accent was placed on their eyes and lips. They were a vision of loveliness. Latoure felt like they were hiding something from him but couldn't put a finger on it. That intelligence training was kicking in again.

Yes, he was going to miss Okinawa—the girls and the nightlife, to be sure. They ate at a restaurant which had a black grill that looked like a pointed hat. You were given a medium-sized bowl and walked down a salad bar filled with all different kinds of vegetables in the first one and an assortment of meats and oils on the second. Jones called it Mongolian barbecue. You picked what you wanted to have grilled, so you had little reason to complain about the food. With a pronounced bang, the cook slapped your bowl on the vertical part of the hot cast-iron grill. With dual spatulas, he mixed and flipped your chosen selection.

You were given a small inverted *V* with a number to place on your table. Rice and drinks were offered as they sat down. The server placed your number where it could be readily seen as the waitstaff passed by. The smell of each diner's selection wafted throughout the restaurant. Very quickly, their table was served each individual bowl along with some hot tea. The meal was very delicious; hardly anyone spoke as they ate. Dinner was completed, and it was time to check out the Club Green Ants.

Both the Restaurant and Club were within walking distance from the *Minshuku*. The music could be clearly heard as they made the last turn down the street toward the club. Latoure felt that it actually sounded very good based on his high school band background. There were two doormen checking IDs; just inside, a woman looked at Latoure and Jones, and reached behind, handing them dark sports jackets. He thought to himself, *This is what the club in LA should have done.*

It was a good thing Latoure asked for $150 from disbursing. Drinks were far from being twenty-five cents apiece like the NCO club, more like the five dollars Jones had told him about for the Buy Me Drink girls. It was decided that like the Club Misty, it would be better to purchase a bottle.

Midori cautioned them, saying, "Buy Suntory Whiskey because that was what in all bottles anyway!" Latoure told Jones. They put Jones's name on it, so he and Midori could come again.

The music was really good and provided him a chance to dance with Michiko. Not just slow dancing, but all the dances of the day. He was very glad his parents made him take dancing lessons during his middle school years. Fox-trot, tango, waltz, jitterbug, cha-cha, plus a dance called "the quick." It was a combination of the waltz and fox-trot. He and Michiko spent a lot of time on the dance floor even receiving applause from some of the other guests. They were a very good match, both as dancers and perhaps more than friends.

Jones and Midori tried a few of the different dances but not all, like Latoure and Michiko had. They did ensure the bottle was not going to waste, pouring drinks for themselves as Fred and Ginger returned to the table as Jones called them. Latoure knew the drink was more whiskey than water and hoped Michiko's wasn't that strong. Time sure flies when you are enjoying the company of a beautiful woman; it was after 1:00 a.m. when the group called it an evening.

Perhaps it was the liquor or tired feet because the trip back to the *minshuku* seemed a little longer.

Jones was a sight trying to remove his shoes, and if it wasn't for Midori's help, he never would have accomplished it. Michiko was slow to put their shoes away, giving Jones and Midori a chance to move up the stairs to the second floor. When she felt they were far enough ahead, she grabbed Latoure's hand for their ascent on the stairs. Halfway up, she stopped a stair above him, placed her hands upon his shoulders, leaned in, and placed the most passionate kiss he had ever felt in his life on his lips. Not just a quick, simple kiss but a chain around his lips to his ears then his neck. When she stopped kissing, those almond eyes stole his heart.

They reached the second-floor landing just in time to see Midori and Jones stumble into their room. The booze was definitely showing its effect on them. He was glad that they had spent the majority of the evening at the club dancing instead of drinking. He was about to slide open the door to their room when Michiko yanked forcefully on his hand, pulling him further down the hallway. When they visited the bath early that day, Latoure never noticed that just to the left, there was an area marked "Showers." This was Michiko's destination for them.

When inside, Michiko turned and locked the door behind them before turning and pointing at the lockers to put their clothes inside, as well as a huge stack of fresh towels. She began undressing him, so he joined in by undressing her. The shelf inside the shower was filled with different soaps, shampoos, and rinses; you name it and more than likely it was there. She definitely had a purpose in mind, pushing and pulling Latoure until she had him where she wanted in the shower stall. Jokingly, she turned on the cold water, driving him up the closest wall as she laughed then added hot water.

Five, ten, or twenty minutes, Latoure wasn't sure how long they spent washing and rinsing one another. There was as much time kissing and caressing as washing. Michiko was more relaxed and freely allowed him to wash, rinse, and kiss every square inch of her body. *Flawless,* he thought, as he finally got a good look at her body not covered with towels, futons, or clothes. She turned the water off as she reached for a towel and began softly drying off Latoure first, then he reciprocated.

Wrapped in towels, their clothes draped over their arms down the hallway to their room. Michiko adjusted the futons the lighting; then allowed the towel to fall to her feet. She reached for Latoure's towel and yanked it off as she moved into his arms. The dim room light washed over her face, highlighting those beautiful almond eyes. As the two kissed deeply, their hands caressed one another's bodies with more purpose than in the shower. Kneeling in front of him, she pulled firmly down on his arms until he was kneeling also.

Latoure placed his arm around her and gently lowered her the remaining distance to the futon. Their bodies melted together in passion; Latoure sensed that Michiko was a little nervous, so he made sure he did not rush. She slowly came out of her shell as they made love again and again, exploring one another. Latoure knew this was love; he never felt like this before with any woman he had been with. If it was wrong, he didn't want to be right. Just before dawn, they fell asleep holding one another.

Around 10:00 a.m., they woke to both Jones and Midori shaking the door and yelling, "Wake up, sleepyheads!" They quickly dressed and opened the door between the rooms. "We have to be out of here by eleven, so get your business done ASAP!" Jones said.

"Will do," they replied as Michiko and Latoure went to take care of their morning routines. Ten minutes later, he was ready, and soon after, Michiko was as well. Their bags were packed, and they went down the stairs to check out. They thanked the person at the front desk and loaded the rental.

They held hands as Jones drove them back to the girl's apartment. Both Marines helped them carry their bags up to Midori's place. Latoure just realized he didn't know where Michiko lived other than somewhere close by. The couples did a quick review of their time together with smiles and laughter.

Then Jones said, "We've got to return this rental. Let's get moving."

Latoure and Michiko hugged and kissed.

She stepped back and said, "Sayonara Larry-san!" That was the first time she had spoken that to him.

He said, "I will stop by the club tomorrow night, okay?"

She didn't answer, but tears began to run down her cheeks as she turned and went farther into Midori's place. He was confused, to say the least, then Jones said, "Let's go!"

Once in the car, Latoure asked Jones, "What was that all about?"

"Open the glove box," Jones replied. Inside was a standard legal-sized envelope with his name on it. Upon opening it and sliding out the paperwork, he immediately knew what it was.

It was his orders for Vietnam; his departure from Kadena was at ten o'clock tomorrow morning. Now he understood the tears and passion Michiko shared for him.

"Jones, you should have told me. I wouldn't have done some of the things we did if I knew."

"The girls wouldn't let me, and I would have been in deep shit with Midori if I did. The only time sayonara is spoken is when you don't expect to see that person ever again," Jones told Latoure.

Latoure didn't quite know what he was feeling; he knew that if he were to stay on the Rock, Michiko would have been a permanent part of his life.

Jones swung by the barracks first, and they unloaded their bags. Latoure rode with Jones to return the rental so he could talk to him in greater detail about what the girls had said or done. What it came down to was that both of the girls wanted to give Latoure some good memories of his time on Okinawa. He told Jones to please tell them both that he would not forget his time on their beautiful island and hoped he could be stationed there in the future. He asked Jones if it would be okay to communicate with Michiko through him, which, of course, was fine with Jones.

Latoure spent the remainder of the afternoon getting his gear all set for his departure in the morning. Jones told him the buses would leave around eight thirty, give or take. Satisfied that there was nothing else to accomplish, he lay back on his rack and stared at the ceiling, thinking about what his future held. Denny stopped by his room and asked if he wanted to go to evening chow with him.

Latoure got up and went with Denny to chow, who said, "I heard you are shipping out tomorrow!"

"Yes, I am. Does everyone but me know?" He was laughing.

After morning colors, Jones stopped by, shook his hand, and wished him well; and Latoure echoed the same to Jones. True to his word, the buses pulled up right at eight thirty and was loaded according to rank, with all their gear placed in the rear of the bus.

As the bus pulled up to the Foster rear gates, murmurs and catcalls echoed in the bus until an officer commanded, "At ease!"

Making the right turn toward Kadena, he saw what all the noise was about. A beautiful girl was dressed in a Kimono, standing close to the Club Misty. In Okinawa as well as Japan, there was a celebration for the coming of age, when twenty-year-olds became adults; they were dressed in traditional clothes. The celebration was in January, so there had to be another reason for this girl to be wearing her kimono. His eyes almost popped out of his head; it was Michiko smiling at him as the bus drove by. A sharp salute was all that Latoure could do without being the center of everyone's jokes. She did a shallow bow as an answer. Her image would be in his brain from this day forward.

Processing at Kadena was painless as all the passengers were mustered, and the Flying Tigers aircraft taxied up. According to rank, all embarked for the short flight to Da Nang Airbase, Republic of Vietnam. Latoure began putting his mind in warrior mode for the flight as best he could, with images of Michiko popping in and out of it. For some unknown reason, the aircraft did a combat landing, which meant it went from ten thousand feet to the deck very rapidly. Tires squealed. He had arrived.

CHAPTER 2

Da Nang: 120 Degrees
in the Shade

They were deplaning by rank, as is the custom for any form of transportation in the military; when Latoure reached the aircraft door, he was met with a solid wall of humid heat right in the face. He had to force his body to take a breath as he moved down the plane's stairs. Off in the distance sat a group of hangars, where he noticed the passengers who deplaned before him were milling around. As he approached the group, he was not saluting anyone, as was the custom in a combat zone, there were about seven or eight tables with a couple of administration clerks processing the arrivals paperwork. There were signs designating which unit the clerks represented. Quickly, he identified the First Marine Division's table and took his place in line.

The admin clerks worked very rapidly; in no time, Latoure was at the front and was presented his orders.

"Oh, you are a spook. You have to report to G-2 Division Headquarters for assignment. I can't do anything for you, Sergeant Latoure. Hop on that six-by-six, second one in, and when it is full, you will be transported to the division."

The seabags and B-4s that were removed from the plane were stacked off to the left of the check-in area. In no time, he collected his gear and then moved to the rear of the truck. Aided by the fellow Marines in the rear of the truck, in no time at all, both he and his B-4 were ready to go, waiting on the last few stragglers headed for the Division.

It seemed like all the Marines and the two navy corpsmen had looks that made one wonder what they were soon to be getting into. Latoure hoped that he wore a look of confidence rather than someone who was unsure of himself.

The six-by-six driver yelled, "We are loaded now, so hang on! The Division Headquarters is just down the road. However, we will be passing through the *World Famous Dog Patch*, for those of you who are interested!"

True to his announcement, ten minutes later, they pulled into the Division Headquarters. On the road, Latoure took note of the area, identifying the Freedom Hill Exchange and Package Store, plus Dog Patch; although he would never visit there. Because he was only a Sergeant, he wouldn't be taking advantage of the Package Store anytime soon.

Headquarters was a heavily sandbagged building, which included a sandbag wall as a protection, which ran the entire length of the building. It created an eerie feeling as one walked down this makeshift passageway. Every door was clearly marked with a wooden sign painted scarlet and gold denoting, G-1 Administration, G-2 Intelligence, G-3 Operations, G-4 Logistics, and G-5, which was an unfamiliar designation to Latoure. He was to learn later in his tour it stood for Psychological Operations. *Let's make it easy on the enemy and let him know which office to attack first,* Latoure thought to himself as he reached the door clearly marked G-2. He created a ruckus as soon as he stepped inside the door. The Marines within were scrambling to find their weapons, thinking they were being attacked by Latoure. From the rear, the command "Stand down" bellowed then "Come back here!"

Working his way around the desks where each Marine was trying to cover what was on them to block Latoure's view. He was glad that he had dropped his B-4 bag at the entrance, for it would have been quite a task to move throughout this unattended barrier. Reaching the desk where the commands had originated, a beautifully carved name in wood read "MGySgt R. D. O'Donnell, Intelligence Chief." Latoure handed his orders to the Intel Chief and stood at attention while the Top read them.

"You must know some pretty important people to get your orders changed like you did, Latoure. Let me have a look at your SRB [Service Record Book]." The Master Guns spent a few minutes reviewing it then added, "So you are an added bonus to the Intel Community, so you get to pick where you want to serve."

On the wall behind the Top were the placards: First, Fifth, Seventh, and Eleventh Marine Regiments; below each of the three battalions, with the exception of Eleventh Marines, only one battalion was listed. The Intelligence Officers were first; beneath them were the Intelligence Chiefs, Map Makers, and Administrative Clerks. None of the names were familiar to Latoure, coming from the I & I staff in Atlanta; in fact, only one other Sergeant could have graduated Intelligence school with him.

Looking directly at the Intel Chief, he said, "Master guns, if the First Marines was good enough for Chesty, I hope it will be good enough for me." (Chesty Puller is the most decorated Marine in history.)

"Good choice, Sergeant Latoure. Gunny Sparks could use you as a Relief Intel Chief and Intel Watch in the Command Bunker. I'll give the Gunny a call on the landline and have him send "Ski" to give you a lift to 1st Marines. Corporal Smith will show you where you can hang out, waiting for him. Corporal Smith, take Sergeant Latoure to the Transit Tents to wait on Lance Corporal Ski."

"Can do, Top!" the Corporal answered.

A short hump down the hill, he went to an area filled with general purpose tents that were aligned and covered down. Corporal Smith pointed to the one clearly designated "Transit." Just inside the tent flap was an empty rack where Latoure put his B-4 bag.

"I will tell Lance Corporal Wajahowski where you are. He is the S-2 driver for the First Marines."

"Thanks, Corporal. Have a great day," Latoure answered.

The stifling heat was getting to him; opening the flap of the tent created a little breeze, so using the B-4 as a pillow, he lay down. In less than a minute, he was asleep, dreaming of Michiko. To say it was difficult to sleep in that heat and humidity would be an understatement. He felt as if he were in a cocoon, floating in limbo of heat and now sweat. The cot rocked, but Latoure failed to open his eyes. The second time the cot was rocked, it almost tipped over. Standing over him was a Marine with a fire hydrant shape and was solid as a rock, to be sure.

"You Latoure?" came the question.

He replied, "Sergeant Latoure. Are you Lance Corporal Wajahowski?"

"Yes, Sergeant, are you ready to roll? NFG," Ski mumbled to himself. Newbies were referred to as NFGs or FNGs, which meant "New Fucking Guy or Fucking New Guy," depending on which outfit you were in.

Ski tried to pick up Latoure's B-4 bag, but the Sergeant said, "I've got it!"

A short hump back up the hill, and he was heading toward the Division Headquarters; there sat an M-151 jeep clearly marked with a wooden plate "First Marines S-2."

"Hang out here for a minute. I have to pick up messages to bring back," Ski said.

"Can do," he replied. As Latoure sat in the jeep, the past few minutes went through his mind over and over. Never again would he allow himself to sleep so soundly. After all, he was no longer on Okinawa; he was in a combat zone. Ski returned, carrying a leather satchel with a padlock, securing it closed.

"No offense, Sarge, but you haven't been checked out yet, so I need to keep this with me." What Ski was telling him was that his clearance needed to be checked before he could have access to the message traffic.

Riding in the jeep, Latoure had a much better view of each area they passed through; they were heading south on RVN Highway 1— the Highway 1 Bridge, as it was called. Ski wasn't speeding, which gave Latoure time to take in much of the surrounding area. Across the bridge, then another ten minutes or so, they arrived at the First Marines headquarters. The First Battalion, First Marines was also at the compound, which was very close to the Village of Dong Tien 2.

They made a left turn into the Regimental area, just off Highway 1, which ran right through the Marine compound. Ski pulled up in front of a hut clearly marked S-2. "Check in with Gunny Sparks if he is sleep then the Skipper, okay, Sarge?"

"Can do. Thanks for the ride," he answered.

"We will be seeing a lot of each other from now on, Sarge!"

In military fashion, like tents at Division, the Huts (sometimes called Hooches) were all lined up neatly in a row, each being 12 by 24 feet. The S-2 was next flanked by the Regimental Aid station and the S-5.

Latoure set his B-4 next to the steps leading into the S-2. Private First Class Henry Hitt was sitting almost in front of the door, slowing down anyone who tried to enter farther inside. A wall about sixteen feet in blocked off the rear. Looking over Hitt's left shoulder, he noticed a Captain whose name Latoure could not read off the nameplate on the field desk where the Intelligence Officer sat.

"Sergeant Latoure, reporting as ordered, sir." Standing at the position of attention.

"Hitt, take the Sergeant over to S-1 and get him started checking in."

"Yes Sir." Was Hitt's reply, which seemed to Latoure was spoken in a disrespectful manner. As a new guy on the block, Latoure let it go this time.

A very short walk across the compound to the S-1 up the steps into the Administration spaces.

"Can you find your way back to the S-2?" once again in that demeaning manner, Hitt asked. "Then I will take you around to check in."

If looks could kill, Hitt would have been lying on the floor; looking back over his shoulder, Latoure only nodded as a reply.

Just inside, a voice said, "Let me have your Service Record Book Sarge." The Admin Chief, Staff Sergeant Stone, requested. Latoure handed his paperwork and SRB to Staff Sergeant Stone, who had offered is hand to shake as a welcome aboard. Right then and there, Latoure knew that he liked and respected Staff Sergeant Stone.

"Half the places on here you don't need to check in with. I'll line them out for you. You will get used to Hitt. He is an arrogant ass. That's why I lent him to the S-2 instead of working here."

"Thanks, Staff Sergeant Stone. Let me get checked in and start doing some work."

Retracing his steps back to the S-2, he picked up both his B-4.

And Private First Class Hitt said, "Let's drop your gear off at the Intel Hut so you don't have to lug it around."

Once again, no respect was given. They passed the Command Operations Center (COC) where Latoure would spend much of his time while he served with the 1st Marines. Wooden pallets were used as walkways so when the monsoons arrived, you wouldn't get mired in mud.

"The Sergeant's quarters are at the other end, you are the only Sergeant in the S-2, so you have it made." It was spoken with jealousy, Latoure felt.

Just as they were about to enter the Hut, or Hooch, referring to what the quarters were called, rounds began spitting up dust all around them. Hitt immediately crouched down behind a fifty-five-gallon water barrel, using it as cover, cradling his M16, and leaving Latoure with no cover and no weapon. Latoure put a boot squarely on Hitt's ass and pushed him down to a prone position.

"Either give me your weapon and hide behind the barrel or let me take cover and you see who is shooting at us."

Not more than four or five minutes, the shooting stopped; Latoure later learned that Mike Company Third Battalion, First Marines was in contact outside the wire about 1,500 meters away, and it was friendly rounds that was impacting the compound.

Hitt got to his feet; his head was hanging down, knowing he had shown his true colors to the Sergeant. "Where do you want to go first, Sergeant Latoure?" he asked.

"How about going to get a weapon, seeing you are afraid to use yours." He couldn't help himself; he had to throw out that dig.

"Sure thing. The armory is right over there." He was pointing about five yards away.

Weapons were issued based on the billet you held, so first was a .45-caliber M-1911 pistol and holster, then an M16 with a bipod and four magazines.

"That all I get?" Sergeant Latoure joked.

"That's it. Unless you are going to be involved in perimeter security," came the answer.

"He is a spook, so yes, he will be," Hitt told the armorer. In that case, he turned around and handed Latoure a Remington pump-action shotgun with two boxes of shells, a fléchette, and a box of buckshot rounds with twelve in each one.

They returned to the hut, where Hitt introduced Sergeant Latoure to a couple intelligence Scouts. Intel Scouts, as they were called, were 0311 Infantry Marines who needed or got a break from serving with an infantry platoon. The job was a little more dangerous because the Intel Scout Team comprised only two Marine Intel Scouts, two Kit Carson Scouts (VC who had been vetted and came to the Allied side), and a spook; in this case, it was going to be Sergeant Latoure since the previous Sergeant had already rotated back to the States. Latoure asked them to keep watch of his weapons while he finished checking in.

One of the two Corporals said, "Welcome aboard, Sarge!"

He pointed at the bullet holes in the screen just above his rack. After what just happened, Latoure opted to put on the .45 and to wear it the rest of the day.

Thanks to Staff Sergeant Stone adjusting his check-in sheet, in no time, he was finished checking in. Latoure turned in his check-in sheet to Staff Sergeant Stone and returned to the S-2.

The Intel Officer told him, "Take the rest of the day to get squared away and report back here at 0800 tomorrow morning. The Gunny and I will figure out what to do with you by then."

"Aye, aye, sir." Latoure backed out of the hatch. He was glad he had time to get some information from the two Intel Scouts, so he had a little bit of an idea what his duties might be.

On the way back to the intel hut, Latoure bought a six-pack of cold Cokes to share with the Scouts. Introductions went quickly; the corporals were Brown and Kirby, and Kirby was an ordained Baptist minister, fresh from Vietnamese language school in Monterey, California.

It was good to have someone other than the Republic of Vietnam interpreters or the Kit Carson Scouts to translate papers and interrogations. Corporal Brown had been up north, and his flak jacket showed he had been in some firefights; a chunk was missing from the back where white stuffing was showing. It was an Army issue, but the Marines always took advantage where they could.

While they were getting to know one another, two Kit Carson Scouts stuck their heads in the screen door. Latoure waved them in palm down, as was the custom; palm up was offensive in the Far East. Brown was the senior of the two corporals, so he did the introductions. Can and Tang were their names, and Brown spoke extremely highly of both. Latoure was later to learn both Can and Tang were North Vietnamese Army Regulars or NVA for short. Policy did not allow for NVA to enter the Kit Carson Program, so these two must have proven their worth to the powers that be. The group of Scouts drank the sodas, laughed, and told stories. Ski joined them; he also lived in that part of the intel hut. Hitt was the odd man out, living in the admin hut.

Latoure gleaned loads of information of who was who in both the Friendly Forces and the Vietcong or NVA. He was more than ready to do his part; he was well pleased with the Scouts. He asked where he could take a shower and was told to go to the huge water towers down by the Eleventh Marines and motor transport areas, about fifty meters away.

"Be prepared. It is cold as fuck," he was warned.

So he grabbed his new jungle utilities, socks, and boots. He wore no underwear; he had already learned that while on Okinawa, to prevent rash. Off to the showers he went. True to their word, it was cold as fuck. Marines are a peculiar bunch whose communication skill involved more swearing than English. Even Corporal Kirby, the Baptist minister, was an offender.

When he returned, a twenty-inch box fan was at the head of his cot, the air mattress was filled, and a pillow and poncho liner were neatly on the cot. He asked the Scouts, "Who do I have to thank for this fan?"

"Your predecessor left it, and we have our own, so it is yours now" came the reply. "Also, Mama-san squared your area away. You and she can work out how much you pay her. We give her five bucks each month. It's a great deal, plus she does laundry too."

He had all the comforts of home with the exception of the cold shower, but he had a plan to remedy that real soon. He found a wooden footlocker she had placed under his cot, and all his gear was neatly placed inside.

Grabbing the M16, which was also under his rack, he began to fieldstrip the weapon to inspect it for cleanliness and any mechanical issues. He spent the next hour cleaning all his weapons; the shotgun had some surface rust, and the .45 had more sand than a seaside beach. He placed the M16 with a partial magazine of fifteen rounds, seated but not charged, on the bipod given to him by the armorer, alongside his rack. After being shot at earlier, he wanted to be prepared. An added bonus that was discovered in his gear was a Marine Corps K-Bar knife. It was sharp enough to shave with and well-kept by whomever had it before him. Satisfied his area was in order, he leaned back; Mama-san had placed his pillow closest to the wall, separating his area from the Intel Scouts. He could hear every word being spoken, and it seemed he was the main subject.

He heard things like "NFG. Still shitting stateside chow. Seemed to have his shit together." And even one of the Kit Carson Scouts chimed in with "He number one, you see."

He got up, flipped the air mattress around, then placed the box fan on top of the footlocker, so it blew straight down his rack. He stabbed the Ka-Bar into the two-by-four above his head. He forgot to set his alarm and rummaged until his clock was found at the very bottom of the footlocker. Setting it for 0500, he felt all was squared away then lay back down. It was almost too quiet the rest of the night; he could hear an occasional vehicle moving along the wire and voices murmuring. Time would tell if he was ready for the next thirteen months in Vietnam, as a restless sleep washed over him.

The alarm rang for three or four seconds and brought Latoure to a total state of awareness in about the same few seconds. Outside the hut, a stand was built with a dishpan on it; he used it to brush his teeth, wash his face, and shave. The water from the five-gallon jerrican was ice-cold. If possible, he would take a walk down to the

Seabees area that very day. The chow hall was in the First Battalion's area. A hearty breakfast of powdered eggs (green tint and all), a couple strips of bacon, some toast, and of course, the lifeblood of the Marines, hot coffee. He did some stretching, push-ups, pull-ups, and sit-ups. After chow, he was ready to get the day started.

Checking his watch, it read six thirty; there was still ninety minutes more or less before he had to report in. He began to walk along the perimeter fence, which ran very close to the Scouts' Hut and his new home. In less than seventy-five meters, he came across the Seabees area; just the people he wanted to see. Luckily, there were three Seabees unpacking some gear, so Latoure approached with a smile on his face.

"Good morning, gents. How's it going, and can I give you a hand unpacking?" All of them wore only olive drab tee-shirts without any rank.

"We got this, Sarge, but no one volunteers to help without wanting us to do something for them, so what's up?"

"Really, I have ninety minutes before I have to check in with the S-2 Officer. Name's Latoure and I wouldn't mind helping at all."

"So you are the new spook on the compound. We heard rumors to that effect," the same Seabee replied.

"Guilty," he answered, while joining the line moving the gear to a staging area.

After all the gear was moved and he exchanged handshakes with all, a cup of coffee was handed to Latoure. The group sat down on whatever was the closest piece of equipment that would hold his weight. The 1st Class Petty Officer one rank senior to Latoure who was doing most of the talking.

"You must be a mind reader because I did come searching for your area." Latoure said.

"I thought so Sarge, so what is it that we can do for you, we've never worked for a Spook."

"Well, I had the pleasure of using the shower yesterday, and my voice still hasn't returned to normal. It is an octave or two above normal." It brought the laughter Latoure hoped it would. He did have a good sense of humor.

"So what were you thinking?" The first class asked.

"Well, you guys are the professionals. What do you think?" The Seabees threw around a couple of ideas. Latoure already had one; using an immersion burner in a fifty-five-gallon drum would work. The Seabees went further than that.

"Okay, we can run a pipe from the tower to the Intel Scout Hut to fill a fifty-five-gallon drum containing an immersion burner set atop a frame with a tarp and swinging door."

"Holy shit, men, that would be awesome. How much will it cost me?"

"If you allow us to use it as well, only one or two AK-47s with the folding stocks. The M16s keep getting in the way when we are using the heavy equipment."

"That's a deal. Let me know when you want to get started," Latoure spoke.

"Today too soon?" he answered.

"Hell no!" he replied.

"Thanks. Got to go to work. Thanks a bunch!"

He stopped by the Scouts' Hut on his ways to the S-2 and told them what was going on with the Seabees and asked where they could get their hands on two AKs with folding stocks.

Brown said, "No problem. All enemy weapons are turned in, up to be checked and tagged. Let me work on it today."

"Outstanding. I don't know what the Skipper and Gunny have planned, but I will try to swing by around chow time."

As he was walking away on the way to the S-2, he overheard the Scouts slapping each other's back and a few "I told you so."

The morning so far had been super, and he wondered what else was in store as he opened the screen door to the S-2. Hitt was at his desk, however, the Skipper and another Marine were talking at the Intel Officer's desk.

"Sergeant Latoure reporting as ordered, sir."

"That is the last time I want to hear that, Sergeant Latoure. This is a combat zone, and we are a little relaxed on formalities."

The Gunny came and shook his hand. "Gunny Sparks here. The Captain and I thought we could use you to get the Order of Battle up-to-date, it's been awhile since either of us had the time to glean documents and message traffic." OOB is the identification, command structure, strength, and disposition of personnel, equipment, and units of an armed force. "We've set up a desk with individual slots for both VC and NVA units we know have or are operating in I Corps." The Gunny continued, "We also think by doing this you will also get up to speed on who, what, where, when, and how the bad guys move about."

Latoure moved to the desk Gunny Sparks pointed to and began to read message traffic, translated documents, plus any other items that might help in putting this kind of puzzle together.

Hitt showed up around 08:30 and was asked, "Where you been at, Hitt? Work begins at 08:00 around here," Gunny Sparks asked.

"I had things I had to do," Hitt answered in a condescending manner.

"You ask first, PFC. You got that?"

"Yeah, yeah, oh so sorry." He was mocking the locals' attempts at English.

Latoure sat there; his blood was boiling, and he was thinking he needed to have a chat with Hitt about respecting his elders and seniors. After three hours of reading traffic, Latoure's eyes felt like they were made of lead, so heavy it was hard to keep them focused.

He almost forgot about his meeting with the Seabees at chow time. Turning toward the Gunny, he asked, "Can I have a talk with you please, Gunny? It will only take a minute. In private please."

"Sure, let's go out back, grab a smoke, and you can let me know what you need," Gunny Sparks replied.

They walked through the S-2, and as they passed the doorway, Latoure noted a cot and gear set up in the room at the rear of the S-2.

"This is where I sleep. That way I can keep track of the comings and goings of who enters the Hooch," The Gunny informed Latoure. Out back, there was kind of a patio area with lawn chairs set up and a small table between them.

"Okay, what's up, Sergeant Latoure?"

"Gunny, I had the distinct pleasure of taking a very cold shower down at the water tank. You will find that I am an act rather than a react Marine. I stopped by the Seabees area, and they will build one complete with immersion burner to heat the water. Right outside the Scouts' Hooch."

"Sounds good. How much money do you need?" the Gunny asked.

"No money at all, Gunny. Two folding stock AKs. The M16s are not suited for their big equipment and really could use the protection."

"That's it? Only two AKs?"

"Well, they want to use the shower also, but nothing else."

"Okay, I have your back on this one as long as I get to use it too?" the Gunny replied, laughing. "In fact, I have four of them under my cot right now. Take two down to the Seabees. Go alongside the hut so the Skipper or Hitt can't see what you are up to."

"Thanks, Gunny." Latoure grabbed the two best-looking AKs and headed toward his appointment with the Seabees.

As he passed alongside the Scouts' Hut, he noticed that the Seabees were already building the shower unit. The First Class saw him approaching and yelled, "Damn, you're quick!"

Latoure replied, "Well, look at you go too!"

The Seabees even ran pipe from the huge water tower right up to the top of the new shower. There would be no need for a bucket brigade to fill the fifty-five-gallon drum. The Seabees thought of everything. Another drum was set close to the unit; it was filled with sand, in case of fire, which was doubtful seeing the burner operated on diesel fuel.

"Here you go, Sailor." He handed the AKs to the First Class.

"Pleasure doing business with you, Sergeant Latoure."

"I have to hit the bricks. Thanks again for the shower."

He went into the Scout Hooch. Mama-san had his area all squared away, so he went into the Scouts' half. The Scouts were still sleeping, so he backed out and headed for chow. It wasn't green eggs this time. In fact it was lunch meat and bread with lettuce and all the fixings. The milk had to have been powdered because it left a chalky film in a person's mouth. The chocolate cake with white frosting was actually very good, despite having to wash it down with powdered milk. As he ate his lunch, he looked around the chow hall for a familiar face; unfortunately, there wasn't anyone he knew. Time to get back to the S-2.

Compiling OOB was much like a word search or puzzle. You found a piece of information on this message, confirmed it with another document, until it all began falling into place. Latoure became focused with his assignment, so much so that everyone else in the S-2 had left for the day; even the Gunny wasn't in the back. He missed chow, but that wasn't his worst problem. No one told him if he needed to lock the door or what else needed to be done to secure the S-2 other than securing the safes containing classified information. Luckily, just as he finished putting all the OOB paperwork in the safe, the Gunny returned with a towel wrapped around his waist. Latoure called back to the Gunny, asking what needed to be done to secure the S-2.

"Nothing, as long as I am around here in back. Other than that, just secure the classified and lock the safes."

"Did you make chow, Sergeant Latoure?"

"No, I missed it. Too involved in this puzzle, Gunny," he answered.

"Stop back here then," replied the Gunny.

Knocking on the doorframe just to make sure the Gunny was dressed, he entered when he heard "All clear!" Just inside the door stood Gunny Sparks holding an unopened case of C rations.

"These should ensure you never starve while you are working here."

"Thanks, Gunny." He took the case of Cs from the Gunny and headed back to the Scouts' Hooch.

He threw the case on the deck, and it made a really loud crash as it came to rest.

Corporal Brown stuck his head through the hatch and asked, "You okay, Sarge?"

"Sorry, Corporal Brown. Got a little carried away with this case of Cs."

"Oh, you missed chow, eh?" Brown replied.

"Sure did," he replied.

"We have a bunch of Cs as well, especially the ones none of us like. Maybe we can work out some trades with you?"

"Sounds like a plan, Corporal. We can do that now if you aren't too busy taking everyone's money." Brown had a reputation as a crapshooter. He had learned that from the Seabees earlier in the day.

"Okay, let me grab our case," Brown answered with a look of wonderment, thinking, *How the heck did he find that out only two days on the compound?* Latoure had learned information was out there for the taking if you only listen for it.

The next thirty days or so, Latoure got into a daily routine of reading intelligence summaries, Interrogation Reports, and Debriefing Patrols, and updating the Order of Battle. One of the debriefs was an Intel Patrol that Corporal Kirby and the 2 Kit Carson Scouts were involved in. Within 1,000 meters of the compound, the Intelligence personnel did patrols almost every evening, taking with them some of the Headquarters people to let them get their feet wet, so to speak. Kirby had just received a letter from his girlfriend, enclosed was a pair of pantyhose soaked in her perfume. He had worn it around his neck that night and was kneeling by a bush when from the other side someone spoke in Vietnamese, "What is that smell?"

Kirby answered, "I smell it also." Taking advantage of his language school training.

As he was replying, he was also rising to his feet very slowly and pointing his M16 at the bush. Unknown to him, the Vietcong on the other side of the bush was also rising and pointing his AK-47 at the bush. Almost simultaneously, they both emptied their magazines into the bush while rapidly backing away from it. There were no casualties on either side except for that bush. It was interesting to note that the VC was that close to the compound; the reason was unknown.

On occasion Latoure accompanied Ski to the division, carrying captured documents and equipment, especially if there was information of real importance contained within. Returning from one of these trips, Ski began to slow down in the dogpatch while telling Latoure, "I have to pick something up for the Gunny."

As Ski slowed, a beautiful girl came rushing up to the jeep and climbed in the back of it. Latoure and Ski exchanged knowing looks with ear-to-ear grins. Just before Ski was to turn into the First Marines compound, he stopped, and the girl scrambled out and made her way through the barbed wire and into the rear of the S-2. Latoure asked Ski how often he carried this special cargo, and the reply was "Around once a week." The girl could be an informant, spy, hooker, or any number of things, but that was the Gunny's area, not his.

Latoure began standing Midwatch, from midnight until 0800, a couple of times a week to get used to operating the KY-38 and PRC-77. Two pieces of radio equipment that when combined became a secured net. It was rapidly becoming a nightly duty, so Latoure had to sleep in the one-hundred-plus heat. He found that a twenty-inch box fan on high came in handy, as well as learning to self-hypnotize himself.

There were two things that further helped Latoure adjust to life at the First Marines. Just like the day he arrived, rounds began impacting the compound and popping the screen above his head. He heard footsteps running down alongside the Intel Hooch, so he rolled from his cot, onto the floor, pointing his M16 at the door, ready to fire at will.

It was Ski shouting, "We are under attack get to the perimeter bunkers and repel the attack!"

Latoure threw on trousers and grabbed the extra magazines; he headed for the Intel-assigned defensive positions with shower shoes and no shirt, just weapons and ammunition. The firefight did not last very long as the command "Cease fire!" was ordered up and down the perimeter. Back to the hut and some much-needed sleep.

The other incident involved Private First Class Hitt. Hitt had continued to disrespect anyone and everyone. Hardly a day went by where Hitt didn't get under somebody's skin. Latoure had just finished his midnight watch and was checking in with the Captain and Gunny, as well as giving them the intelligence summaries he copied that evening. For whatever reason, Hitt tried to push Latoure out of the way with a body block.

Latoure turned to Hitt and said, "What is your problem, Private First Class Hitt?"

"I don't like you spooks. I don't like Ski, and I especially don't like you. In fact, if you weren't wearing those Sergeant's stripes, boot, I would kick your ass with all my karate training."

What Hitt didn't know was Latoure was a Black Belt in the Okinawan Isshin-Ryu style of karate. His cousin learned this style, which was primarily a hard-striking technique, while serving in the Navy. He was a Sensei (Teacher) in Upstate New York and had gave Latoure many lessons before he joined the Marines. Looking into Hitt's eyes, Latoure removed his jungle utility shirt on, where his metal Sergeant's collar rank were worn.

"Let's go, Hitt. You sure you want this?"

Hitt looked toward the Captain, hoping that he would intervene, but the Captain rose up and told Latoure he would return in 5 minutes he was going to grab a smoke also, the Gunny was at Division with Ski. The Captain already knew that Hitt had it coming and that Latoure was more than capable of defending himself and that it was clearly outlined in Latoure's SRB.

"Out back, Hitt, follow me," Latoure ordered.

First, he passed through the screen door, and as Hitt drew abreast of him, he grabbed a handful of Hitt's family jewels, picked him up, and threw him facedown in the sand. Latoure didn't want to turn this into a karate match, just put Hitt in his place. As Hitt scrambled to his feet, he rushed the Sergeant. Sidestepping the charging private first class, this time he grabbed his belt, lifting him up and dropping him back facedown in the sand. Latoure sat on Hitt's back and slapped the back of his head three or four times. As he did this, he said, "Use this brain for something other than a hat rack, Hitt."

With little effort, he picked up Hitt, turned him around to face him, and waited to see Hitt's reaction. "I'm sorry, Sergeant Latoure. I was wrong."

"Then prove it, Hitt, show me you can be an outstanding Marine," Latoure told Hitt.

They both entered the S-2. "Tell the skipper I am sacking out."

"Yes, sir," Hitt answered.

He replied, "Don't call me sir."

CHAPTER 3
First Marines: The First Ninety

Latoure began to learn about the ins and outs of life in the First Marines, plus all the superstitions of what might happen, which was believed by almost everyone in-country. One of the main superstitions was that if you were going to be wounded, it would happen during your first ninety days or your last ninety days in-country. So just in case, Latoure circled June 22 with a smile on his face. Another superstition was you never eat the apricots in and around the tanks, especially ensuring the tank crew didn't see you if you did. There were others, but those were the two that he put to mind.

After the counseling session with Hitt, the private first class did a marked turn around. He even began to bring his guitar to the S-2 and played for everyone; he actually was a very good musician. His songbook was actually quite eclectic. Ski was busy plotting identified enemy units on the S-2 map. The map was a 1:50,000 scale of Da Nang and the surrounding area. It had to be updated daily before the First Marine Commanding Officer's daily briefing. Latoure and Ski were the ones tasked with standing the midnight to 0800 Intel Watch within the command operations center (COC). Latoure did five days, and Ski did the remaining two, which gave Latoure time to update the order of battle.

The COC was currently in the middle of a communications upgrade, so midwatches, as they were called, was being handled by a minimum crew; both had a day off, so they decided to do the Intel run. The date was April 27, 1969. For any service personnel who was stationed in and around Da Nang, it would be a day to remember. They had just crossed over the bridge on Highway 1, about two miles from the left-hand turn through the Dog Patch, leading toward Freedom Hill and the Division Headquarters. The road in front of them seemed to rise up by two or three feet just before the high-pressure concussion wave from exploding ordnance struck the jeep.

ASP-1 (Ammunition Supply Point 1) was exploding, created by a fire that was intentionally starting to burn down brush or a VC sapper, depending on who you believed. The M-151 jeep strap ran along Latoure's right side that kept him from being ejected. He loosened the strap enough so he could lean out and scan the sky for the falling bombs and artillery rounds. The explosions were sending ordnance everywhere, exploding when it impacted the ground. To say the entire area was in a state of chaos would have been an understatement. Latoure would yell "STOP or GO", depending on what was falling in and around them. Ski did an outstanding job of operating the jeep, and they arrived at Division Headquarters unscathed.

The bombs had not exploded around Division; most were falling further down Freedom Hill. Grabbing the leather satchel, he began walking quickly down the sandbagged corridor to the G-2. He had just reached the door and opened it an inch when a 250-pound bomb detonated at the entrance to the walkway. The concussion wave funneled down the passageway sought the least path of resistance, the door that Latoure was opening. The force was so intense that it picked up Latoure off and pushed him across the floor on his stomach, about fifteen feet. The Intelligence Chief's desk was the reason he didn't slide any further. The Intel Chief stood and looked over the top of his desk, saying, "You okay, Sergeant?"

"Shit, Ski's outside!"

Scrambling to his feet, he ran back outside after throwing the satchel on the Top's desk to check on Ski, who was nowhere to be found. He began searching the area and found Ski at the other end of the Headquarters building. He had moved the jeep into the shade at the far end. The spot where Ski had dropped Latoure off was now a crater about three feet deep. Ski was in the middle of his tour, not being affected by the first ninety or last ninety days superstition, so it seemed.

He quickly returned inside and announced, "Ski's okay!" while picking up the satchel that had been filled with returning intel traffic. "We are out of here, Top!" He was leaving in a hurry to return to base.

It was a repeat of the trip to Division, with Latoure hanging outside the jeep yelling Stop or Go, depending on what was falling from the sky at that particular moment. It was about a five- or six-mile trip from the Division back to the Highway 1 Bridge, which Ski made in record time.

The Marine Sentry stopped them, saying, "The Bridge is closed. ASP-1 is blowing up!"

Latoure was always proud of the fact that he communicated without the use of foul language; however, in this case, he lost his temper. "Where in the Fuck do you think we just came from? Were we transported here by the Starship Enterprise? We just drove through the bursting bombs, and we want to return to 1st Marines. Call the Sergeant of the Guard, Officer of the Day, or the Commandant to give us permission to pass."

"Okay, Sarge, settle down. I am only following orders." He walked over to the checkpoint bunker and rang up the Officer in Charge on the field phone. In less than a minute, they were cleared to cross over and headed south on Highway 1.

Of course, everyone wanted to hear what was going on up north; between Latoure and Ski, all were brought up to speed. It was amazing that the jeep came through it without a scratch, considering how close to the jeep the ammunition detonated on the return trip. Latoure attempted to research the cause for ASP-1's catastrophe, to no avail. Later in his career, he was stationed with an ammunition tech who was there and learned it was caused by locals, not Marines, trying to burn down the overgrown brush that would have hid anyone trying to sabotage the ammo dump.

It was a basic rule that Intelligence personnel did not stand any type of duty because they had a myriad of other tasks to stand like the Midnight Watch in the COC. However, the Intelligence Officer— who Latoure later learned was not a primary 0202, meaning career Intelligence Officer, but holding a secondary MOS of intel—did not want to kick over the apple cart and volunteered Latoure for Sergeant of the Guard during the month of May. It was a onetime deal, never to happen again. There was no use in trying to argue, so when the May Duty Roster was published, there was his name on Mother's Day, May 11th, 1969. Ski and Latoure adjusted their COC watches so he would be available on the eleventh. He took advantage a couple of days ahead of his duty assignment to walk the inside perimeter, checking out all the bunkers, towers, and other areas that would fall under his responsibility as Sergeant of the Guard.

First Battalion was assigned to the Dong Tien 2 compound and manned all the bunkers during daylight, but during the overnight hours from 1630 to 0800, most were manned by Headquarters personnel from both the Battalion and Regiment. Then at 0800, they were relieved by First Battalion grunts once again. He felt comfortable after his rounds of the perimeter on whose area was whose, plus the passageways through the concertina wire, which ran along Highway 1, leading to the posts. He had the duty roster for Mother's Day in hand, accompanied by the two Corporals of the guard; formation was held at 1615. Not wanting to rock the boat too much, assignments to specific bunkers were done according to the previous days. The M-60 machine guns were manned by Marines from the Weapons Platoon and were evenly spread out along the perimeter.

The was no reason to believe anything was going to happen, especially because Latoure had access to message traffic and the latest locations of all known enemy units within I Corps. The Officer of the Day was a newly assigned second Lieutenant awaiting assignment to one of the three Battalions. He was an Infantry Officer and was willing to listen rather than demand his way or the highway.

The evening went by uneventful; that is, until around 2230. Post 7 had heard something outside the wire and called over the field phone, "Sergeant of the Guard Post Number 7."

"I'll let you know what I find out and might as well do a perimeter check after seeing what is up at Post 7," Latoure told the Lieutenant.

He replied, "Take the M14 with the Starlight scope. You will be able to see outside the wire better with it."

"Aye, Aye Sir" and he headed out for Post 7 with the M-14 in one hand, his issued M-16 on the other, plus the .45-caliber pistol on his hip. He never wanted to be without some protection, so his armament included a bayonet, k-bar, and pilot's survival knife with sharping stone; he was loaded for bear but moved to Post 7 alone in the pitch-black night.

Post 7 was an M-60 post manned by Machine Gunners from the Battalion's Weapons Platoon; professional grunts, not headquarters personnel, which gave more credence to the report.

"Give me a boost up on top of the bunker so I can scan the wire with this Starlight," Latoure asked. On top, he was handed the M14 then his M16. He crawled to the front of the bunker and whispered down to the Machine Gunners, "I need a couple sandbags to prop this M-14 on." Quickly, his request was honored. Both Marines inside the bunker were as eager to know what they heard; Latoure understood their concern because he felt the same.

Deliberately, he began to slowly scan the fence directly in front of Post 7 outward. Ten yards to the left was Post 7 Alpha, a tower about twenty feet high. Moving the Starlight in a slow arc, he caught movement at about one o'clock from his position. He finished scanning a complete 180-degree arc before returning to recheck that one o'clock area. There was a bomb crater close to the local's cemetery, where he felt the movement originated; inside the crater were five sappers.

He immediately knew they were sappers by their lack of clothes and the explosives strapped across their chests. He slowly moved to the rear of the bunker and dropped down. He spun the handle on the field phone and informed the lieutenant, "We've got sappers outside the wire!"

In a professional manner, the Lieutenant answered, "You're shitting me."

"Wish I was, LT, but I am not. I plan on keeping them pinned in the bomb crater where they are hiding until you can send out the Reactionary Platoon to grab them. That sound OK?"

"Rodger, keep me informed, Sergeant Latoure."

"It won't be me. I am on the top of the bunker, looking down on them, so the Post 7 Marines will relay."

"Got ya. Let me get going. Out."

It's not a radio, LT, he thought to himself as he once again was boosted up on top of the bunker.

The sappers routinely went to the compound that they planned to attack the night before, where they cut the wire and taped it close. On the night of the attack, they yanked open the wire and rushed through, throwing satchel charges in all the bunkers and any target of opportunity. The five sappers were still there, lying on their backs; if the sun would have been shinning, you would have thought they were trying to catch a tan. He felt a hand grab his left calf by whoever it was pulling themselves up on top of the bunker. It was the First Battalion's Executive Officer, Lieutenant Colonel Vreeland, who asked, "What you got, Sergeant Latoure?"

Latoure whispered, "One o'clock, sir. Five sappers in that bomb crater." He was whispering below, "Hand me up another sandbag for the XO." Quickly, that was done.

As they continued to watch the sappers, alternating between the sappers and scanning the rest of the wire, one of them reached inside a bag and pulled out a cat. He squeezed it roughly, causing it to meow very loudly. Holding the cat's arms extended above his chest, he continued to make it meow.

"Watch this, Colonel. Shot out."

The reason this was said was to allow the XO time to close his eyes so the Starlight wouldn't blind him when the muzzle flashed. Latoure had placed the round directly at the cat's head; it meowed no longer. The XO chuckled and said, "You are a sick puppy, Sergeant Latoure. What's the status of the React?"

Latoure whispered down and had the Marines contact the Officer of the Day to answer the XO's question. The reply came back, "He's at the south gate with the react ready to roll."

The XO whispered down, "Tell them I said Execute."

The sappers must have heard the react coming or one of their own told them, but they were attempting to crawl out of the bunker. The XO told Latoure, "Don't let them get away, Sergeant."

"Shot." Latoure placed a round in front of the sapper that was the farthest out of the crater, who quickly scrambled back into it. A second sapper tried to use a tori-style marker as cover, but a tori is like an upside down "U", giving Latoure a clean shot and hitting the sapper in the thigh. He wasn't trying to kill the sappers, just keep them in place until the React Platoon could capture them.

The React Platoon had made it less that fifty feet outside the perimeter when an RPG (Rocket Propelled Grenade) streaked toward Tower 1; the second RPG flew toward 7A. Both towers had NODs (Night Observation Device), which were basically huge Starlight Scopes. The location of those NODs only could have come from someone who worked inside the compound. That would have been the only way the sappers would have known to target those two towers and none others. The XO's place was at the Command Center, not acting as a spotter for the Sergeant of the Guard, and left soon after the RPG struck Tower 1. Latoure thought it was probably safer to be inside the bunker rather than on top, so he began to move to the rear. His lower torso was hanging beneath the top of the bunker just as the third and final RPG struck the front of the bunker, impacting on the middle of three sandbags, which comprised the roof. Just like the bomb going off when ASP-1 denoted, the concussion blew him off the top of it and rearward about thirty feet, impacting the sandbag and retaining wall with a thud.

He wasn't as lucky as he was at Division; this time, shrapnel peppered his lower legs. It didn't hurt until he attempted to move; then a quarter-sized piece, which was stuck in his shinbone, moved when his trousers tugged on it. He couldn't see it that well, but he definitely felt it when he tried to move. Reaching down, he found the protruding piece of metal. Gingerly, he grasped ahold of the shrapnel and yanked it out, much like pulling out a child's tooth. He wasn't in any pain, so he moved back to Post 7. The majority of the RPG shrapnel and concussion went through the bunker; both Machine Gunners lay motionless on the floor. The landline was gone, blown apart. The M-60 appeared serviceable, and Latoure manned the weapon.

Condition 1 was well on the way as other Marines quickly scrambled out to their assigned positions, engaging the sappers. One of them didn't have a weapon; he was going home in the morning and had turned it in to the armory.

"Take my M16. Drop it off at the Regimental S-2 in the morning."

"Thanks a whole bunch. Semper Fi!"

Another Marine joined him in the bunker who became his A Gunner. Then five or six Marines took up fighting positions in and around the bunker for the rest of the night. In the midst of the battle, it occurred to Latoure it wasn't the day before the attack, as he had first thought, but actually the real attack.

During the chaos of the attack, the night's sky was filled with what seemed like a thousand gigantic flashbulbs originating at the 81-millimeter mortar pits. The mortarmen were alternating between high explosive and illumination rounds. All night they kept up their mortar fire, which detonating rounds outside the perimeter which stopped the Sappers dead in their tracks or light them up for the Marines, including Latoure, to concentrate fire upon the Sappers. The Marines did what they do best and engaged the enemy.

An OV-10 Bronco came on-station, meaning it circled the compound, directing artillery fire from units stationed at other compounds. Despite the artillery and the Marines' fire, Sappers were getting very close to breaching the barbed wire. The Bronco rolled in parallel to the Marines' line and let loose with over a dozen 2.75-inch rockets. Latoure watched the rockets streaking toward the lines, not in a straight line but moving to and fro. He could feel the heat when the rockets exploded and said a silent prayer that the rockets would be on the outboard swing when they impacted. Of course, they were, and he got to meet and also serve under that OV-10 pilot who became an F-4 Phantom Squadron 312's Commanding Officer eight years later with Latoure as his intelligence chief.

As all this was happening, Latoure, his A gunner, and the six Marines around Post 7 continued deadly fire at the sappers trying to breach the wire directly in front of them. It was touch and go for quite a while. At one point he saw a sapper directly in front of the bunker stuck in the wire. He fired the M-60, and in a flash of light, the sapper was gone. Latoure's small group continued to fire at targets of opportunity for the remainder of the night.

Around first light, Latoure handed over the M-60 duties to the A gunner who, in fact, was a Machine Gunner by trade. If Latoure had known that, he would have handed the M-60 over to him. Feeling confident with what little remained of the night and the early morning glow beginning to shine, the M-60 was in good hands. Neither of the two Marines who had made the initial call that evening survived the RPG blast. Latoure was very fortunate the blast went down and not up. Assisted by the Marine who he lent his weapon, respectfully, they placed the bodies outside the bunker, so they were no longer underfoot. Latoure would notify the Corpsmen who would honor the fallen even more.

Directly in front of Post 7 lay the bodies of thirty-nine enemies, all killed by 7.62 mm rounds and not by M16 rounds. Two sappers almost breached the wire; their bodies were entangled in the constantia. For this action, he was awarded the Personal Vietnamese Cross of Gallantry from the country of Vietnam. The rumor was that the Battalion XO had also submitted both the Lieutenant and him for a Bronze Star.

He toured the guard posts one last time before returning to the Guard Shack, ready to report to the Guard Officer his findings. Staff Sergeant Fletcher, the First Battalion Intelligence Chief was talking to the Lieutenant as Latoure approached, overhearing, "We have to check the bodies for documents and stuff." As he turned and noticed Latoure entering the shack. "You're with Regiment, aren't you?"

"That's right, Staff Sergeant Fletcher. I am," Latoure replied.

"The Sergeant and I will handle it. Can I take him with me?" Staff Sergeant Fletcher asked the Lieutenant.

"You stand relieved, Sergeant Latoure. Outstanding job last night. I would serve with you anytime." He was filled with pride at the Lieutenant's comment.

As Staff Sergeant Fletcher and Sergeant Latoure walked away from the Guard Shack, Fletcher asked, "In or out?"

"What the heck does that mean?" Latoure questioned.

"You want to check bodies or do you want to cover me from inside the wire?"

"Seeing I have been up all night, I would like the inside, if that's all right."

"Sure, no problem. Where's your M16?"

"I loaned it to a grunt last night. It should be at the Regimental S-2."

They walked together toward the S-2, discussing how they would work as a team. His weapon was there with a ten-dollar MPC note taped to it. "The Marine who left it was very grateful."

Gunny Sparks said, "So he made it. That's great. He was going home today."

Staff Sergeant Fletcher added, "I am going to borrow Sergeant Latoure to check bodies, okay, Gunny?"

"Go for it. He's off today anyway," the Gunny replied.

It was becoming routine as Fletcher checked bodies, putting anything he found in a canvas burn bag before moving on to the next one. From time to time, Fletcher would take a Polaroid as Latoure's eyes scanned all around the Staff Sergeant, looking for movement. A Marine Corps M-48A3 tank was standing guard at the southern entrance, preventing any traffic from entering or exiting the compound. The two walked shoulder to shoulder across Highway 1, moving toward Eleventh Marines section of the compound and the last section that needed checking. About halfway through the Eleventh Marines, Latoure noticed, out of the corner of his eye, one of the sapper's head was now facing in a different direction than when he first checked it. Now it was looking at Fletcher approaching the sapper. Ever so slowly, he was moving his left arm along his side and reaching for what, Latoure did not know. When Fletcher was less than five feet away, the sapper did a push-up, jumped to his feet, and began running away from the fence line and ultimately Fletcher.

Latoure screamed out, "Hit it, Fletch!"

And the Staff Sergeant dived to the ground. Every one of the Marines who were still manning the bunkers and defensive positions opened fire on the fleeing sapper a millisecond after Latoure screamed out. Marines are known for their marksmanship; however, if the sapper was hit, he didn't fall. A small hut made of cement blocks was about five hundred meters outside the compound; just as the sapper reached the doorway, the 90 mm main gun of the tank fired a fléchette round. The building disappeared in a green haze, taking the fleeing sapper with it.

Latoure moved back down to the southern gate after the search had been completed. Staff Sergeant Fletcher was reviewing the Polaroids of the sappers. He held one out to Sergeant Latoure, asking if he recognized the sapper.

"Shit! Staff Sergeant Fletcher, that is or was one of the barbers!"

"You got that right. Never trust anyone, even the KCSs." Then he told Latoure to swing by the First Battalion's S-2 later that afternoon after he got some sleep.

"Is 1500 okay, Staff Sergeant Fletcher?"

"Sure. See you then," Fletcher answered.

His leg began to throb. He had forgotten about the wounds in his lower legs until just then. He thought it wouldn't be such a bad idea to swing by the Regimental Aid Station and have one of the Corpsmen look at his legs. During his month and a half, Latoure had gotten to know the corpsman really well, often playing contract bridge with them. The Naval Air Station's Commanding Officer's daughters had taught him how to play. In fact they were such good teachers that he became the fourth for many of the Base Commander's bridge games.

Gingerly, he stepped up and into the aid station; the dried blood had made his jungle utility trousers stick to his leg. Bill, the corpsman who was Latoure's normal partner, noticed the blood stains and asked, "What happened to you?"

Latoure answered, "I got hit last night while standing Sergeant of the Guard."

"Drop your trouser. Let's have a look." Latoure hesitated. "I know you jarheads don't wear skivvies. We don't either. Drop 'em."

He didn't need any stitches. There was a deep cut where the piece was stuck to his shinbone and many small holes oozing blood. Doc, as the Marines called the Corpsman, worked swiftly, cleaning up both legs and putting two new bandages over the deep cut. Butterfly stitches, he thought Bill called them.

Bill began filling out a casualty tag, which was the first step in submitting for the Purple Heart. He noticed what Doc was doing and asked, "Listen. I have only been in-country less than ninety days. I don't want this to be the reason I have to leave Vietnam." The rule was if you have three Purple Hearts, you were required to leave. "Besides, Doc, Purple Hearts are for those who lose arms and legs, in my opinion."

"Okay, it's your call, but keep a close watch on your legs. If they begin swelling or turn red, come back," Bill told Latoure.

"Thanks, Doc. I got to get some sleep. I am bushed."

As he passed the S-2, he yelled that he was going to hit the rack, and the reply "Go for it" came from within. He really wanted to take a shower, but that would have washed all the medicine Doc had just put on his legs. He threw his jungles in the corner where Mama-san told him to, if he wanted things washed; he slipped on his running shorts, turned the box fan on high, and was asleep before his head hit the pillow. His rack began shaking, and Ski was telling him Sergeant Fletcher had called the S-2 looking for Latoure. He told Ski, "Ring him back. Tell him I am on my way please." He walked outside with a washcloth and bar of soap, and gave his upper torso a quick wash.

He arrived at the First Battalion's S-2, entering the office thirty minutes late and hoping he wasn't in too much trouble with Staff Sergeant Fletcher, who yelled, "Come out back, Latoure!"

So he stepped back outside and walked along the side of the S-2 to the rear. Fletcher had a very nice set up, including a BBQ grill constructed from half of a fifty-five-gallon drum; on it were two steaks.

"Cop a squat!" Fletcher told him as he handed Latoure a cold Black Label beer. "I had to thank you for saving my ass today, and this is what I came up with."

"Hell, this wasn't necessary, Staff Sergeant Fletcher. I was just doing what any other Marine would have," he replied.

"That's right, but many wouldn't have done it as fast as you did. I could hear those Eleventh Marines' small arms flying over my head. You were outstanding, and once again, thanks." So the two intelligence men drank beer and ate steaks, talking about stateside.

The documents recovered from the dead sappers disclosed they were from the T-69th Sapper Battalion. Latoure looked at what order of battle information he had filed on the unit. It listed the strength as sixty-nine sappers, with the last known location farther up the A Shau Valley. The total number of enemies killed were sixty-six, meaning the T-Sixty-Ninth no longer was an effective fighting force. Latoure's wounds healed very quickly while he continued his daily routine of either COC watch or working on the OOB.

Something was revealed after the sapper attack; usually the RVN interpreters lived and slept in their assigned hut along Highway 1. Not a single interpreter was on hand the next morning, which led the Marines to believe they had prior knowledge of the attack. Latoure filed that information in the back of his brain, to be used if necessary. Little did he know that in two weeks' time, he would.

When he initially checked in with Master Gunnery Sergeant O'Donnell, the Division Intelligence Chief had told him that Latoure was going to be utilized as a relief intel chief when the three that were assigned to the Battalions of the First Marines were relieved, going on rest and relaxation (better known as R&R), or needed to be replaced. Such was the case with the Second Battalion's intelligence chief, who was rotating, and a replacement was required for an upcoming operation.

CHAPTER 4
Second Battalion, First Marines: Operation Pipestone Canyon

He checked in with Second Lieutenant Garcia, the Battalion's Intelligence Officer, who was fresh from Intelligence School, making him a career, not secondary MOS spook. Because of the marked absence of the interpreters after the Mother's Day attack, Latoure had asked and was given permission to take one of the Kit Carson Scouts along with him to the Second Battalion. Both Can and Tang argued with one another on which one would go with him. Not understanding that much Vietnamese, even Corporal Kirby's formal language school couldn't follow along at the rate of speech the Scouts were talking. Can won the discussion and was standing beside him when introductions were made. It struck Latoure as funny when people who were supposed to be allies couldn't be trusted, as was the case with the interpreters; while Kit Carson Scouts, who were Chu Ho to the Marines, could.

Pipestone Canyon was designed to take away the Vietcong's safe havens of Dodge City and Go Noi Island, which were located approximately ten to twenty kilometers southwest of Da Nang. Marine, ARVN (Army Republic of Vietnam), plus Korean Marines were involved. The operation was to begin May 26, 1969. The Lieutenant, Latoure, and Can ended up riding in a UH-34 helicopter headed south to join the operation. As the helicopter made its approach to the landing zone, it did a slow spiral of 180 degrees. Latoure was the first one out as the tires reached the top of the elephant grass. It was a tooth-jarring landing because the elephant grass was over eight feet high. The Lieutenant took off in the wrong direction because he didn't have the advantage of looking out the window to witness the 180-degree turn the helicopter made.

Latoure was yelling over the noise of the chopper, "Garcia, Garcia, hey, you!" It was to no avail as the Lieutenant kept heading off in the wrong direction. Finally Latoure screamed out, "Lieutenant!" It froze Garcia in his tracks. Normally you never discussed rank in the field nor salute, but it had the desired effect as he turned and headed back toward Latoure.

Someone way above the Lieutenant and Latoure's pay grades had made the command decision to cover the Intelligence Net. It was a dedicated frequency for disseminating Intel and Intel Only. Prior to this operation, Intel was carried by PRC-25 radios alone, which wasn't a cipher-capable radio. So now they were upgraded to PRC-77, and the KY-38 ciphered system had two radios instead of one. The KY-38 had to be punched daily with a key punch at the same time of day every day in order to communicate. The two communication devices were mounted on a packboard, leaving Latoure almost no place to put his personal gear. Can carried the Sergeant's personal equipment, food, socks, and such, plus his own. Latoure carried the Remington shotgun and the .45 pistol.

They broke into a clearing below the landing zone, into an area which resembled a marshaling area for heavy equipment. Marine Corps Amtracs and Tanks plus Bull Dozers and a myriad of heavy equipment operated by the Seabees were all in different parts of the staging area. The kicking off point was the northern most border of what the Marines called Dodge City. Within this enemy stronghold, the brass expected to find both enemy units and tons of their weapons and equipment. A U-shaped blocking force was set in place. Looking south, an RVN Battalion was assigned the southernmost point; the left flank was the South Korean Marines; then finally two Companies of the Second Battalion on the right flank. All the assignments were to act as a blocking force, ensuring the enemy remained trapped within the U.

The Lieutenant set up shop inside one of the Amtracs, where all captured enemy equipment could be tagged, as well as an area to do a field interrogation of any captured Vietcongs. The units assigned to sweep ahead of all the heavy equipment began moving out, with Latoure and Can closely behind. When an area about five hundred meters in front of the marshaling area was clear of the enemy and booby traps, diesel engines began to roar. Their task was to strip off the top six inches of dirt, burying anything in their path. If the sweeping units contacted the VC or found caches, that information was radioed back so the equipment could slow down or even stop.

The undergrowth, trees, and bunkers were cleared by all units involved in the operation. Almost daily enemy weapons and equipment, if not the Vietcong themselves, were brought to the S-2, where the Lieutenant, Latoure, and Can tagged and field interrogated them. Field interrogation was done to find out the who, what, where, when, and in what direction the enemy units before them were headed. Latoure was lucky that it was Can who assisted in the interrogations because Can could definitely get what information was needed without any problem, especially if the Lieutenant and Latoure stepped around the Amtrac for a five-minute smoke break.

Every evening, when defensive positions were put in place, Can found an excellent area for Latoure and him to bed down. Can had brought five hammocks for them to use, while the lieutenant slept inside the amtrac with the capture equipment. The prisoners were flown out by helicopter to the rear echelon daily, where they faced a much more thorough interrogation. Before Latoure got to take advantage of what Can had set up, he had to radio in the Intelligence Summary (INSUM for short); it was written by either the lieutenant or Latoure, depending on who was privileged to the most info of that day's events. Combat rations or C-rats provided their daily substance, while the mosquitoes ate their fill every evening as well; one and all ignored them as best as they could.

The Lieutenant and Latoure took turns guarding the captured equipment as well as riding in the Amtrac. Latoure much preferred to do an active part, sweeping the areas in front of the slow-moving operation. He was becoming more confident being in enemy territory, especially with Can's guidance on what to look for and where to look for booby traps. Additionally the signs which pointed directions to caches or bunkers by piled rocks or sticks. It came to the point that if there was enemy presence, the hair on the back of his neck would stand up, warning him in advance. About two months into, the operation in Dodge City was almost complete, opening up Highway 4 from Ho Ann to Hill 65 without the threat of enemy attacking it at will.

The daily routine was far from being boring; each day brought something new, either through interrogations, a discovered cache, or enemy documents. Nightly, as he radioed in the Intelligence Summary, the traffic he received back contained words of encouragement and what the Marines called "attaboys" for a job well done. Both he and Can took turns walking point for the amtracs. The majority of the friendly casualties were from booby traps rather than firefights.

Latoure did not want to prejudge anyone or any unit for that matter, but just like the absence of the ARVN translators during the Mother's Day attack, the AVRN blocking force was like a sieve. It was estimated by the fixed wing and helicopter aircrews, which maintained a watch overhead during daylight hours, that up to three hundred enemies escaped through the AVRN blocking force. Those enemies who chose to try either the left flank met the Korean Marines, or those at the right flank enjoyed a welcome by the US Marines. In either direction, the enemy found the going a little more difficult.

Sixty-five days into the operation, the Song Thu Bon River came into view; across it lay the next target—Go Noi Island. The Marines took the time to bathe in the river while the Seabees finished up leveling Dodge City behind them. The water was chilly but afforded them a chance to wash off months' worth of sweat and dirt. The operations had to slow down because the last few acres of Dodge City were filled with a myriad of caches and hidden bunkers. Latoure was still amazed that the Seabees were clearing over 250 acres of land down to a depth of six inches daily. The captured enemy documents, weapons, and equipment filled the amtrac almost to the top. A decision had to be made on what to do with it.

The solution was that Lieutenant Garcia would accompany the vital pieces of equipment and documents via helicopter to the rear for further inspection then return the following day. The remaining would be Latoure's responsibility to destroy. It was determined that task would be completed once the amtracs crossed over the river to Go Noi Island. Because of his previous training when he first joined the Marines, Latoure felt confident that destroying the enemy equipment wouldn't be difficult. Little did he know it wasn't going to be that easy.

Both he and Can had time to clean up both their clothes and their bodies in the river while the Seabees were hard at work finishing up Dodge City. The Seabees also wanted the opportunity to clean themselves and service their vehicle before tackling Go Noi Island. The Battalion Commander gave all a forty-eight-hour stand-down time to get ready for phase 2 of the operation. Defensive perimeters were set to avoid any surprises, but one and all enjoyed a chance to relax and catch up on letters from home.

The Landing Craft arrived to transport the heavy equipment across the river, but first, the Marine Corps Amtrac's engines was racing, and it plunged into the river and rose on the opposite bank of Go Noi Island. Marine units disembarked and established a beachhead just like one would see in the movies. When the area was secure, the signal was given to bring in the heavy equipment and the Seabees. The entire operation went off without Murphy adding his two cents. The defensive perimeters was set this time; more than a watchful eye was kept that night because this was enemy territory.

The time spent leveling and searching Dodge City gave the Vietcong ample time to prepare for the Marines' arrival, and they set about this task in earnest. They had more than tripled the placement of explosive booby traps, plus the nonlethal ones of punji sticks or deadfalls. To say that both Latoure and Can took extra, special care while walking point on Go Noi Island would have been an understatement to say the least. Once again, Latoure was very thankful for Can's tutelage.

When equipment began clearing the island, Can told Latoure that the units were moving too quickly and that many hiding points were being missed. Latoure took Can to see the lieutenant and explained what he was talking about. Can explained that the southern banks were catacombs with entrances leading under the island, into passageways and underground bunkers much deeper than the six inches which was being cleared. The lieutenant told Latoure to go check out what Can was talking about and report back.

"Do you want me to get some Grunts to go with you?"

Can began shaking his head. "No, too much noise. We go, Sergeant!"

It is hard to explain to those who haven't been there, but a special trust is built up when you serve in combat with another person; such was the case between Latoure and Can. They headed toward the southern bank, always watchful for booby traps plus signs showing the enemy which trail to take and which to avoid. They had traveled about an hour when Can tapped Latoure on the shoulder and pointed at a small rise in the bank. They approached very carefully with silence. Latoure could see the entrance about eighteen inches under the water; as he leaned in to inspect it closer, a Vietcong leaped from above with knife in hand, aiming for Latoure's jugular. Can, thinking quickly, kicked the VC in the side, causing the VC to move slightly, so the knife just missed Latoure's throat.

The VC ended up between the Sergeant's legs, facing away, but trapped Latoure's shotgun. Thinking fast, he grabbed the Ka-Bar fighting knife, which every Marine cherished, and plunged it in the top of the VC's head. A second VC tried to join the fight but was quickly discourage after watching his fellow VC's fate and scrambled up the bank, running away. Latoure's shotgun was still trapped between his legs by the VC he had killed, so quickly, he released his pilot's survival knife and threw it at the VC. It was not like you saw in the movies; his survival knife struck home in the VC's back and began waving up and down as the Vietcong fled, as if to say so long to Latoure.

Latoure turned to Can and gave him a bear hug, thanking him for saving his life.

Can pointed to Latoure's neck and said, "You bleeding."

To which, Latoure replied, "Let's dee-dee, Can!"

Their return trip was quicker because during their search, the bulldozers had moved closer. Walking up to the Amtrac, Lieutenant Garcia's eyes bugged out of his head. He yelled, "Corpsman!"

That was the first time Latoure became concerned for his wound. Luckily, his corpsman friend Bill was the one who answered the call.

"It isn't that deep, but you will have a small scar there for life, I think."

"Hey, Bill, like before, if you can." He was referring to the casualty tag. Bill just nodded his answer of yes.

When bandages were applied to wounds in combat, they always seemed to be one hundred times too big for the task.

"How the heck am I supposed to turn my head with this thing on my neck?"

"Give it twenty-four hours, a chance to heal a little. I will change it up tomorrow, okay?"

"Do I have any choice?" Latoure replied, laughing.

The lieutenant interrupted the mutual admiration. "Let's go see the CO."

Can started to walk away, but Garcia said, "Hold up, Can. You are coming too. You are going to back up Sergeant Latoure's brief. Understood?" Can shook his head in agreement.

The Lieutenant went into the command Amtrac and whispered to the CO, who immediately turned to everyone in the Amtrac and bellowed, "Everyone out now, except the intel people."

Thirty seconds later, the trac was empty. "Okay, what do you have, Lieutenant?" Just about the same time, he noticed the huge bandage on Latoure's neck then added, "What the heck happened to you, Sergeant?"

Garcia replied, "It is better if they explain what they found and what went on, sir."

"Let's hear it then."

Can and Latoure spent the next five minutes briefing the CO, who then said, "You mean we have passed up the enemy?"

Both Can and Latoure shook their heads in the affirmative. "Jesus H. Christ!" Then he yelled out the rear of the Amtrac for the

Operations Officer. "Put a halt to operations and order them all back to the initial staging point on the island where we kicked this off."

"Aye, aye Sir!" The Major replied.

Continuing on, the CO said, "How the heck are we going to fix this?" He was speaking out loud rather than asking a question.

"Sir, if I may. Sergeant Latoure came up with a great idea," the Intel Officer told the CO.

"What's that, Sergeant?"

"Sir, what if we could get the Brown Water Mike boats to patrol in conjunction with our sweeps. If the VC try to use the river to double back, the Navy can dissuade them, I bet."

"What's your name again, and what unit did we get you from?"

The Lieutenant the told the Colonel, "Sergeant Latoure and Can here are both on loan from the Regimental S-2. And if I may, an outstanding addition."

"You two, take the rest of the day off. You definitely earned it."

"Aye, aye, Sir!" Both men turned and left the Amtrac, leaving the lieutenant further discussing what happened that day.

Can and Latoure began retracing the battalion's movement back to the kickoff point; however, after what happened earlier that day, to say they were more diligent would have been an understatement. As they passed by the Seabees, the Senior Chief came up and asked Latoure why they were moving back to the kickoff area.

Latoure told the Chief, "Let's just say we missed a bunch of bad guys."

"What are you talking about, Sergeant?" the senior chief asked.

"Let's leave it at that."

Can and Latoure set up camp close to the same area they did when the operation began. This time, there were no trees to hang the hammocks. Opening some C-rats, they ate and talked about that day's experiences, and once again, Latoure gave a heartfelt thanks to Can as well as a pack of Marlboros, which he just about had to twist Can's arm off to get him to accept the pack. Garcia caught up with them about an hour later and told them the CO was very pleased and requested the two of them to sweep along the south bank with the navy, handing Latoure the frequency for the Mike boats and their call sign.

The next morning, Latoure sought out the corpsman to have him remove that huge bandage. Reluctantly, Bill did what Latoure asked, replacing it with gauze and tape directly over the cut, which had stopped bleeding the previous evening. Thanks to Can's quick action, the cut was just a little deeper than one would get shaving. Then the radio began chattering, calling for Red Devil 2 from Fast Mover Actual. That meant the Mike boat commander was calling him.

Latoure radioed. "We can go covered if need be, Skipper." He was letting the Navy know that he had the capability of a secure net. They both went covered and set up how the southern bank was going to be searched. Latoure added that Can would be with him and not to confuse him with a VC.

The entire time the radio traffic was being passed, Latoure and Can were moving toward the south bank. They arrived there just about the same time as the Mike Boat, which pulled bow into shore so Latoure and Can could hop aboard. Latoure saluted the colors then requested permission to come aboard. Everyone shook hands as the boat slowly reversed then moved along the bank, returning to the area where Latoure and Can had made contact. Can pointed out how the Sailors could recognize an entrance to Go Noi. Plus he added what other means the VC would use to show other VCs the entrances. Once the information was passed, the bow moved back into the bank so Latoure and Can could step ashore. Latoure saluted the Chief and requested permission to go ashore; then the national ensign was flying aft of the Mike boat. Both he and Can were happy to be back on land, where they could rely on their own instincts rather than the navy's.

The combined operation lasted about three weeks; the southern bank was now only eighteen inches high, which didn't afford the VC a way to tunnel into Go Noi. The Battalion Commander used the Intel Net to thank the sailors for their help and mentioned he would be passing on to their CO a job well done. By this time, over a third of the island was cleared down to that six inches, and operations returned to normal, if it could be called that. During this time span, the Amtrac now was full of captured enemy equipment, and something needed to be done about it. Lieutenant Garcia asked if Sergeant Latoure could blow up the equipment, to which Latoure replied, "Sure. No problem."

There was a shallow pit created as the bulldozers cleared part of the island. All the captured equipment and explosives were piled in it. Can and Latoure waited until the amtracs and heavy equipment were well on their way out of the area. Latoure had acquired a twenty-pound satchel of C-4 plastic explosive to destroy the equipment, plus about twenty feet of detonation cord to wrap everything up in a neat package to blow sky-high. Can stayed with him to watch his back while Latoure went to work to ensure everything would be destroyed. He slipped the time cord into a single blasting cap then into a block of C-4. Latoure pulled the starter, and the time cord began to burn. He thought it would take around three minutes before denotation, giving him and Can plenty of time to get downrange, away from the blast. They headed off toward the direction the amtracs took.

He checked his watch. Three minutes had passed with no explosion, then four, then five, then six. Something wasn't right; it should have exploded by then. He looked at Can, who shrugged his shoulders. Latoure knew he had to go back and check; if he didn't, it would fall back into VC hands. He told Can to stay way back as he slowly approached the enemy equipment. As he moved closer and closer, he thought it might be best if he did a low crawl the last ten feet or so. If the C-4 blew, it wouldn't matter in the least. Looking at his watch, over twenty minutes had expired, so he felt pretty sure he was safe. There was a small berm surrounding the equipment, and Latoure, as if moving in slow motion, looked over the edge. He had only put a single primer on the C-4, and one-fourth of an inch before the blasting cap, the primer cord was broken. He removed the blasting cap and replaced the single primer with a double one this time.

While all this was happening, two things were as well. The first was the Amtracs were motorized; meaning, with the thirty minutes wasted, they had moved a great distance from Latoure and Can.

The second, night was rapidly approaching. Any person who had done any time in Vietnam knew the night belonged to Charlie, a nickname for the VC. He pulled the primer on both, this time with only two minutes, so he and Can moved away from the cache very rapidly. The ground shook and a huge, black O-shaped ring filled the sky as the enemy equipment exploded. Can, with a huge smile on his face, gave the Sergeant a thumbs-up.

They didn't want to move too quickly trying to catch up with the amtracs for fear of tripping a booby trap that any VC could have set and that was moved in behind the amtracs. The Seabees had already shut down for the evening, leaving about a one-fourth mile between the dozers and the Amtracs. The security Platoon for the Seabees had already begun laying out their positions as he and can passed through. They hadn't traveled more than a couple hundred yards when a small mound appeared in front. Most likely it was a burial mound from a family long since departed in Go Noi.

Can went left, and Latoure went right, moving around the grave mound. Both nearly jumped out of their boots because a couple of Marine grunts thought it would be funny to place two Vietcong KIAs leaning against the mound. Neither of them fired at the enemy, although they were just a hairbreadth away from doing so. He made note to tell those behind of the whereabouts of the two KIAs.

As he approached, the Lieutenant then stood and said, "Damn, you could see that smoke ring from miles away. I guess the VC now know we are ruining their parade." Latoure thought better of letting the Lieutenant know what took so long but did inform him of the two VC bodies. "I'll do the Intel Sum tonight. You and Can go take the rest of the night off. Latoure thanked Garcia, while he and Can went looking for a place to eat and sleep that evening.

The remaining three weeks that Latoure and Can were attached to the Second Battalion passed without any significant actions. Both the Battalion Commander and Lieutenant Garcia thanked them both with handshakes and pats on the back.

"I can't get you a helo out of here. The best I can do is loan you my jeep for the ride back to the regiment," the Battalion Command told them both.

They thanked the Colonel and hopped in his jeep. Latoure wasn't that comfortable riding back, and he could tell that Can wasn't either. Both men had their heads on swivels, looking for signs of enemy presence. Once they left Highway 4 and turned left, heading north on Highway 1, they could relax a little. Both military and civilian vehicle traffic ran this route unimpeded. Latoure was looking forward to a hot shower and a good night's rest on his cot. He slapped Can on his back and told him to take the week off as Latoure turned and walked into the Regimental S-2. Both the Captain and the Gunny were busy working diligently on something, so he just announced, "I'm back. See you in the morning." The Gunny just waved to him, not really paying any attention to Latoure, so he left with thoughts of that hot shower on his mind. As he passed the Scouts' half of the hut, he requested, "Could someone crank up the shower please?"

"Sure thing!" came the answer.

After almost ninety days in the bush, as it was called, the initial hot shower only removed the surface dirt. He knew that it would take a while until his body was cleansed and his pores dumped all the dirt inside. Nonetheless, the hot shower was a good beginning; next would be a good night's rest.

It felt like he had just closed his eyes when Ski began calling to him, "The Captain and the Gunny need to see you this morning, Sergeant Latoure."

"What time is it, Ski?" he asked.

"Just about 0900."

"Shit! I will be right there as soon as I shave, Ski. Please let them know I will be there by 0915."

"Can do and welcome back!"

It was a cold shave, but Mama-san had laid out a fresh set of jungle utilities for him. Dressed and ready, he headed out to report back in.

The Captain and Gunny were bent over, looking at something on the Skipper's desk. In the Marines, a Captain was called Skipper; that is, if he was respected by his men.

"Sorry, I slept in, Skipper."

"That's okay, Sergeant. From what was reported to me, you represented the 2 with honor and integrity. Step over here and take a gander at what we have discovered."

He moved to the captain's side and looked at the OOB map. Ski must have been really busy because all the units which were located far up north in I Corps were now all around within ten clicks (a click represents one-thousand-meter grid) or so from Da Nang. The Q-93 VC Battalion was within five thousand meters of the First Marines headquarters.

"Something big is going to happen," Latoure said, stating the obvious.

The Skipper and Gunny laughed in unison. "We know you just got back, but we have to step up our perimeter patrols. "Brown is getting short, and Kirby doesn't have that much experience yet. So you have to pick up the slack." Brown was rotating within thirty days.

"No problem, Sir. When?" Latoure replied.

"Tonight," the Skipper said. "Take whoever you want to accompany you on the patrol. Five-man team."

"Yes, sir, I'll get it set up now." Just like that, he was back in the middle of the war.

CHAPTER 5

Return to the First Marines: The Perimeter

Tang was waiting for Latoure with news that Can was returning that afternoon, and Can said he would be upset if he were left out of the patrol. Latoure nodded his head, acknowledging Tang. In his mind, that meant he only needed two Marine Scouts to complete the patrol. Walking alongside the intel hut, Kirby yelled through the screen, "Hey, Sarge, wait up!"

Latoure already knew what that was about; Kirby wanted in as well. "Okay, you're in, Corporal. Who else wants in?"

"Well, Ski wants in. Brownie will take the COC watch, so Ski can join us plus. The Gunny approved it."

With that information, the patrol was manned. Now for the weapons breakdown.

"Corporal Kirby, I want you to carry the M14 and Starlight. Can and Tang, M16s, plus Ski with the blooper." The Blooper was the nickname for the M-79 40 mm grenade launcher. "I'll carry the Remington shotgun and my .45. At 2230, we will brief the patrol in your half of the Hooch. I am going to take a nap. Wake me up around 2200, Corporal, please."

"Will do, Sarge," Kirby answered.

As he laid back upon his pillow, Latoure wasn't really concerned about the patrol that evening. He had done it a half dozen times before being sent to Pipestone Canyon, with no incidents to speak of. It felt like he had just closed his eyes when Kirby yelled, "It's 2200, Sarge!"

The patrol briefing took about thirty minutes; the five-paragraph order called SMEAC—which stood for situation, mission, execution, administration or logistics, and command or signal—was covered in detail. They all had done the perimeter patrol so many times before it was second nature; however, with all the enemy movement being reported, there was a good chance this patrol would be far from previous ones. Latoure told Ski that he would be carrying the PRC-77 without the cypher KY-38. That meant Ski would also have a .45 pistol along with Latoure's. Latoure would be walking point, carrying the shotgun, followed by Can with an M16. Kirby, without his girlfriend's perfume-scented nylons, was next with the M14; one time was enough, shooting at talking bushes or Kirby. Tang was next with an M16, and finally, Ski with the radio and blooper. All carried their personal preference of different types of knives; they were armed and ready. Four Check Points were designated at each corner of the compound where the patrol would check, ensuring the COC could monitor the patrol's movement. They headed out to the jump-off point at the north gate of the compound on Highway 1.

The entire compound was lit up like a busy shopping center back in the States; it would be difficult to disguise the patrol's movements until they were at least five hundred meters out. Latoure, knowing that their movements were being watch by either VC or VC sympathizers, decided to change up the patrol route just a little. They headed north on Highway 1 for over a click (one thousand meters) before heading right, leaving the highway and curling back through the jungle, using the foliage as cover. The detour added thirty minutes to the patrol, but he felt it was time well spent, masking the patrol's intended movements.

They hadn't traveled five hundred meters toward checkpoint 1 when the hair on Latoure's neck began to tingle while his palms were sweating. Those warning signs served him well on Pipestone, and he wasn't about to ignore them now. He raised his hand, signaling the patrol to halt. He began to look around and felt something brush his jungle utility pants. Looking down, he notice the trip wire lightly brushing his trousers and slowly eased back a few inches. Can noticed the wire at almost the same time Latoure did. He moved to the Sergeant's side; then using his hands lightly, Can followed the wire first to the left side, where he found the anchor point. He moved around Latoure very gingerly and followed the wire, finding an M-26 grenade pin pull slipped inside an empty C ration can. The booby trap now identified, it was decided to leave it in place so Charlie wouldn't know the patrol had passed this way. One at a time, each member stepped over the trip wire with the guidance of Can and moved fifty feet down the trail until all had passed it.

They were not traveling more than a hundred meters more down the trail when Latoure's senses began to warn him once more. He thought he saw movement out of the corner of his left eye, in the tree line. The trail broke the tree line off to the right, where the patrols normally went, following the trail that spiraled down into the valley below. This was the path the patrol wanted to take, but something wasn't right. Latoure motioned for Kirby to scan the tree line for enemy movement using the Starlight scope. After the sweep with the night observation device, Kirby shook his head in the negative; he did not see anyone or anything.

Off to the patrol's left was the Village burial mounds. Each family's plot was a pile of dirt about two feet high and four feet across. Latoure moved into the cemetery, scanning left and right for movement. In war, sometimes you are lucky, and this was the case that night. Just as each member moved behind a grave mound, the tree line burst with enemy small arms fire not more than thirty feet away. The close proximity caused the VC to fire almost straight up into the air over the patrol's heads. Latoure emptied his shotgun, moving left to right across the enemy position, knowing that the buckshot and fléchette rounds would cause the enemy to duck, giving the patrol time to take up firing positions. As he reloaded the shotgun, the patrol put down a wall of lead to their front. Latoure was pissed at himself for emptying the Remington. His plan was to fire only four rounds and replace them with the rounds he was holding between his fingers; instead he lay there with an empty weapon. This went through his mind as he reloaded, thinking what if the enemy attacked; when you were in close contact, time seemed to almost stop in reality. Not more than ten seconds passed, his weapon was reloaded. The enemy had broken contact; Tang saw them taking off down through the valley.

Ski had already notified the command of the contact and in which direction the VC had scurried off. Latoure told Can to take point, knowing that he could move the patrol much quicker. He told Can that he wanted to beat the VC to the entrance of the valley. Can, shaking his head vigorously, understood and took off with the patrol trying to keep up with his pace. As they moved, Latoure thought that if the enemy was waiting in the area of checkpoint 1, what awaited them at checkpoint 2, the sand dunes in the southwest corner of the compound. The patrol set up an ambush and waited for the enemy to appear from the valley in front of them. Ski had radioed in that they were waiting for the VC to join the party.

About five minutes after they set up the ambush, the Vietcong broke the tree line about one hundred meters from their position. All knew to wait for Latoure's shotgun blast before opening fire. He had to give the VC credit; they were not walking in a straight line; they were moving like a snake, slithering from 75 meters to 125 meters from the ambush. Latoure was waiting for the next leg, which would bring them to within seventy-five meters, but the enemy straightened out their route unexpectedly to a point one hundred meters away. The shotgun blast lit up the night's sky, and the patrol opened fire. Marines are taught to fight through an ambush, but the Vietcong chose to turn and run back down into the valley, dragging their wounded with them. Not knowing the total strength of the VC, Latoure thought it would be best to move to checkpoint 3. But the patrol had a problem.

Both Can and Tang's M16s were jammed; the bolts were locked forward with no cleaning rod to unjam the bolts. Down two weapons, Latoure made the radio call to inform command. Whoever was in charge wanted them to continue the patrol with almost half their firepower depleted. Luckily for them, the battalion XO, Latoure's spotter on Mother's Day, overheard and took charge. He told Latoure to move the patrol to a point about five hundred meters south of the compound, and the XO would arrange for replacement weapons. Latoure told the rest of the team the plan, and they headed out, covering the 1,500 meters to Highway 1 with Can and Tang now armed with Ski's and Latoure's .45-caliber pistols.

As they approached Highway 1, rat patrol (M-151 jeep with twin M-60s) was heading north toward the compound. Noticing Can and Tang's rat patrol and believing them to be VC, they opened fire on the entire patrol. Latoure thought if they could have heard of the M-60 machine gunfire and Ski's screaming into the radio with calls of "CHECK FIRE! CHECK FIRE!" they would have stopped sooner. As it were, about two minutes of M-60 rounds flew over the patrol's head before they finally ceased fire. The patrol carefully moved alongside the jeep, using it to mask their movement as it headed toward the compound. A mule which looked like an early version of a four-wheeler came flying toward them, meeting both the Rat Patrol and the patrol about 250 meters from the gate. The mule driver's eyes were bulging from his head; he was looking left and right, knowing this was no place for him. He was in a hurry to return to the compound. Quickly, the weapons were exchanged for the jammed M16s, and more ammunition for all was handed out. Latoure knew that the driver was very happy that he was to be escorted back by the Rat Patrol to the safety of the compound.

Just as the patrol's rapid movement placed them in a position in front of the VC to ambush them, the weapons exchange afforded the VC time to move ahead of the patrol and were waiting to give the patrol some of what they had just received at checkpoint 2. Latoure felt it would be a prudent idea to alter the patrol's normal route, just in case. The enemy was definitely in the area this night.

The patrol hugged the tree line close to where the tank had blown apart that building on Mother's Day. Just as they were about to report their position at checkpoint 3, the tree line off to the left three hundred meters or so away erupted with enemy fire. The patrol's position was beside the 81 mm mortars within two hundred meters more or less, and wanting to help, they fired illumination rounds. Then following Ski's fire mission, they dropped three high-explosive rounds in the trees hiding the VCs to the patrol's left front. Just as quickly as the firefight began, it was over.

In Latoure's mind, there had to be a reason why his small five-man team was involved in so much contact. They checked out the tree line for enemy casualties, but true to form, they always carried off their dead and wounded. What would be waiting at checkpoint 4 would be anyone's guess. Latoure had a thought and halted the patrol. He went to Ski and made the following radio call. "Eagle, this is Eagle 2 Alpha."

"Go ahead, 2 Alpha."

"Request Tower 1, do a NOD scan of northeast sector for enemy movement, over."

"Roger, 2 Alpha, wait one."

The patrol took advantage of the time to check weapons, reload, and drink some water.

"Eagle 2 Alpha, this is Eagle base."

"Eagle base, this is Eagle 2 Alpha. Go ahead."

"Tower 1 reports negative movement, over."

"Roger that, 2 Alpha out."

At least they weren't heading into another ambush, or so it seemed.

The remainder of the patrol went off without any further contact, as if three out of four checkpoints with contact wasn't enough. As the patrol entered the North Gate, one and all took on a more relaxed mannerism, glad that the night was finally over. Can and Tang were in deep conversation while the Marines were placing one foot in front of the other, looking forward to sleeping the remainder of the night away. Latoure had to report to the command center with the patrol report; waiting for him was Lieutenant Colonel Vreeland.

"What the hell was going on out there, Sergeant Latoure?"

"Hell, I wish I knew, sir. The first contact wasn't AKs, but the contact by Check Point 3 definitely was!"

"I need you and your men to retrace your patrol route at first light and see what you can find out, Sergeant Latoure." This was the Colonel's request, which actually was an order.

The only possible reply was "Aye, aye, sir."

"Look for anything and everything when you go back out. Let's see if we can identify who is checking us out."

Latoure nodded and headed for the Intel Scouts' Hut with the news. The patrol could get almost three hours of rest before having to move out again. Latoure told the Scouts it had to be them to retrace the patrol's route; no one else knew the way they went. This made it easier for the Scouts to understand why them.

Latoure's eyes snapped open at five o'clock; he went into the Scouts' half and said, "Off and on."

No one had taken off their jungle utilities, so it was just a quick weapon's check and off they went again. Because the daylight was rapidly approaching, it was much easier to see where they were stepping. They quickly arrived at the booby trap discovered the previous night, and this time, it was disarmed. Further along, they searched the tree line where the enemy had ambushed them at Checkpoint 1. Blood trails and a single .30-caliber M-1 carbine casing was found. Not a weapon of choice for the VC, but it was, however, a weapon used by the Provincial Reconnaissance Units (PRUs). Was it a case of mistaken identity?

Checkpoint 2 revealed more blood trails and some drag marks leading toward the Village about 2,500 meters away. Could it have been the Village's Reaction Force that they were in contact with. Latoure talked to both Can and Tang to get their input. They were thinking along the same lines as he was. Such was not the case at checkpoint 3. There were definitely bad guys here; AK-47 casings were scattered throughout the tree line. Blood-soaked bandages were also collected along with the AK casings. Tang even found an NVA belt and buckle stained with blood; carved on the inside was the owner's name and rank.

Can told Latoure, "Trung úy belt!"

So it was NVA or at least VC with an NVA advisor with them whom they had contact.

The patrol searched the tree line, which paralleled the east side of the compound, looking for signs of enemy activity. Either Can or Tang began pointing out observation points along the route where the enemy had lay down and observed activities along the eastern fence line. There were four such observation points about one hundred meters apart. It was impossible to tell if it were four different teams or just one team moving to the four positions. It seemed the patrol had ruined the enemy's observation plans for that evening, thus the contact, which more than likely gave the observation team a chance to get away.

Before turning in his patrol report to the Battalion Executive Officer, Latoure went to speak to his boss, the Regimental Intelligence Officer. Things began to fall in place with all the movement in and around the I Corps area, especially close to Da Nang. The Captain told Latoure that he would accompany him when he briefed the XO. After the briefing, there were more questions unanswered than answered. The XO told them he would get in contact with the PRU Commander but doubted that the Commander would take ownership of the contact last night. As for the NVA being in the area, the XO was going to send some First Battalion Platoon-sized patrol sweeps to see what transpired.

On the way back to the S-2, Latoure asked the Captain if it would be okay if he put in for some R&R; rumor central had it that four quotas for Hong Kong were coming down this month, and he would like to put in for one. The Captain approved and gave Latoure the rest of the day off, saying Latoure looked really whipped, which he was, after the previous night and early morning duties.

Staff Sergeant Stone, the Regimental Administration Chief, asked Latoure if he had gotten run over by a water buffalo or a truck because Latoure definitely looked like he did.

Latoure, laughing, just said, "It's been a long night. What do I have to do to put in for R&R?"

"You just did. All you needed to do was tell me. I keep the roster for R&R requests, so there is no hanky-panky going on."

Some shady admin types had been known to sell the prime R&R locations but not Staff Sergeant Stone; he was an outstanding Marine as far as Latoure was concerned.

"Thanks, Staff Sergeant. I need some sleep. Are we playing bridge tonight against the squids?" Stone and Latoure had a weekly game against the Regimental Corpsman.

"Yes, I think we are. See you then," Stone answered.

Walking along the outside of the Scouts' Hut, it sounded like a thunderstorm with all the snoring going on. It wouldn't be very long before Latoure added his baritone snores with the Scouts. While he was sleeping the day away, one of the Sergeants—Smith was his name, who was the head cook at Marble Mountain chow hall—called the Regimental S-2, looking for him. Hitt didn't know how important it was, so he came and woke up Latoure with the message. Latoure thanked Hitt, telling him that he would call him back as soon as possible, ASAP for short. He took a cold shower, which felt invigorating considering it was already one-hundred-plus degrees outside and not much cooler even with the box fan blowing on his head.

As he stepped into the S-2, the Captain asked, "Can you do the Division Intel Run tomorrow and drop Brownie off at Da Nang so he can catch his flight back to the world?"

"It would be an honor, Skipper."

He picked up the landline and asked to be patched through to Marble Mountain's Chow Hall. Even in the middle of a foreign country, less than a minute later, he was talking to one of his old Sergeant buddies from the Staging Battalion. Sergeant Smith told Latoure that he was receiving a shipment of lobsters from a friend living in Massachusetts. And he was positive that at least one or two had Latoure's name on it. Latoure asked the Skipper if it would be all right to swing down to Marble Mountain for a side trip after dropping Brownie off. The Captain told him it was no problem. Latoure told Smith he would see him tomorrow afternoon.

For the remainder of the day, Latoure got his personal equipment squared away, took a hot shower, and got himself ready for that evening's bridge game. Stone and Latoure finally beat the Corpsman that evening for the first time. He thought to himself, *First, lobsters, and now this. Things, they are a-changing.* As they departed the Regimental Aid Station, Latoure noticed voices coming from the rear of the Regimental S-2; it seemed like he would have another passenger to drop off in the morning as well.

Brownie was packed and ready, with his seabag in hand, they walked together to the S-2 to pick up the intelligence jeep. He shook his head as he once again looked at that First Marines S-2 red-and-yellow plaque on the front of the jeep. *Let's tell the whole world who we are,* he thought. He was also right when Gunny Sparks told him to swing around back on his way to the Division, meaning Latoure would be dropping off the Gunny's sweetheart. Loaded up with the satchel and Brown's seabag, shotgun, and .45 pistol, they made a short stop at the rear of the S-2, picking her up, then off they went. Latoure stopped in the Dog Patch, letting off the Gunny's Girl down the road and up to Freedom Hill and the Division Headquarters; satchels were exchanged on the way to drop off Brown. Brownie took about three seconds to grab his gear and go check in for his Freedom Bird home.

Because of his duties in the Intelligence world, he wasn't worried about the trip down Vietnam Highway 538 to Marble Mountain. It was less than a five-mile trip south of the Da Nang Airfield to Marble Mountain; the security noticed the S-2 First Marines plaque on the front of the jeep and waved Latoure onto the base. The chow hall was easy to find, and upon entering, he was told to go out back because Sergeant Smith was waiting for him there. They shook hands and slapped each other's back while Smith pointed to a table set up for four. Latoure thought, *Why four?* But just then, two more of his fellow staging battalion Sergeants showed up.

Smithy put on a feast of all feasts; after meals of C-rats, midrats of baloney sandwiches on COC watch, plus green eggs and ham. The First Marines chow hall thought they were in heaven. It wasn't just the lobsters, although they were awesome, but Smithy had come up with New York strip steaks as well. Sweet corn and rolls rounded out the meal. It was nice getting together with his fellow Sergeants from the Staging Battalion plus sharing war stories of their Vietnam experience.

Latoure's meal was interrupted when a messman came up to him and said, "Division Intel's on the hook for you."

"I'll be right back," he assured his fellow Marines.

Master Gunnery Sergeant O'Donnell was on the line and told Latoure he needed a big favor from him and had already cleared it with the Regimental S-2. It seemed a trip farther south to the

Hoi An MACV compound needed to be made, and Latoure was the closest Intel Type in the area. His duties were to pick up another Intel Type along with the equipment he was escorting and return both to Division G-2 ASAP. Latoure was more than a little concerned about having to make the fourteen-mile trip alone. He rejoined his fellow Sergeants and told them he needed to take off to Hoi An. Once again, his luck held; Sergeant Fowler was assigned at Hoi An, so he asked if he could ride with Latoure. Now Latoure felt a lot better knowing he would have someone riding shotgun, as it was called. The two shook hands, slapped backs, and started their journey south.

Fowler recommended staying on Highway 538 along the coast rather than the shorter route, which would take them through Indian Territory, as it was called. It was daylight, so that trip might have been all right, but why take the chance when the coastal route was definitely safer. On the trip south, Fowler pointed out places of interest historically and places of recent conflicts. The fifteen-mile route went much too quickly, plus with Fowler's guidance, the drive through Hoi An went off without any difficulty. Latoure dropped Fowler off at his quarters, shook hands, and told him to stop by the First Marines and look him up if he ever was in their (Tactical Area of Responsibility) TAOR for short.

Latoure parked in front of the MCV Headquarters, dusted himself off, and went up the stairs. He was greeted by the Guard and asked who or what Latoure was there for. The Guard had seen him drop off Fowler and felt he wasn't a threat.

"I'm here to pick up someone for transport to the Division Headquarters," Latoure informed the sentry.

He replied, "He's waiting at the S-2 for you, Sergeant. Down the passageway on the right, third door."

Latoure thanked him and entered the building. As he opened the door to the S-2, four sets of eyes locked on him. "Sergeant Latoure. I am here to give one of you a lift to the Division."

"That would be me, James Hardy." He offered his hand to Latoure. Hardy was wearing clothes that were meant for an African safari rather than the Vietnam Conflict. It was similar to the Marine

Corps Jungle Utilities; however, Hardy's was a light tan. Latoure took note that no rank was offered.

"You will have to spend the night here, Sergeant Latoure, but that will give me time to show then teach you what we will be bringing to the Division."

"No problem, sir." Latoure thought it was more prudent to add the sir.

"Listen, Jim will be fine when it is just you and I. Hardy when others are around."

"Got you, Jim."

"Follow me," Hardy told the Sergeant.

They walked out the rear of the MACV Headquarters to a locked CONEX box. Hardy worked the combination of the Sergeant and Greenleaf lock, of which Latoure was very familiar. The S&G was the standard lock for securing classified during the Vietnam War.

Once inside the CONEX box, Hardy knelt down and worked another S&G, this time on a reinforced footlocker or a locker similar to one. As the lid was lifted, Latoure noticed a dozen or so metal boxes about the size of a lunch box, but each with a key sticking in it and a couple of dials.

"These are called SIDs, which is short for Seismic Intrusion Device. These are Phase 1, with many for Phases to follow. I am the person who is the manufacturer's Technical Representative." That explained the clothes Hardy was wearing. "Please understand both the equipment and its use are classified Top Secret Need to Know. You and your Intel Scout Team are the talk of the town and have been chosen to deploy the SIDs around the Division TAOR. This locker is filled with different types and are only an example of what the SIDs can do."

Latoure knelt down beside Hardy, who explained the ins and outs of each sensor. Not only were these sensors that recorded seismic activity but a myriad of other things. The key was used to arm the sensor once engaged; if moved, a small charge destroyed it. For the next hour, Hardy explained each sensor and its use, which he had brought from Stateside. Hardy also told Latoure that deployment wasn't scheduled to begin right away rather three months hence.

Hardy added the fact that a BPU, standing for Balance Pressure Unit, had already been deployed close to Hill 10. It was basically two garden hoses running parallel to each other. When walked upon, a signal was sent of the activity.

When the briefing was completed, Hardy said, "Let me buy you dinner." After the steak and lobster lunch, Latoure really wasn't that hungry but knew he couldn't say no.

During the course of dinner, Hardy talked of his family, the protests in the States, and current events that the Marines in combat did not hear of or really care about. Latoure was stuffed and wanted to know what time they would head out in the morning. Hardy told him there was no rush and that he looked worn out, which wasn't an understatement.

"How about 09:00?" Hardy said and showed Latoure where the head and showers were, plus the sleeping quarters. You would have thought after the day's activities, Latoure would have been asleep soon after his shower, but his mind was going over what he had just learned and what would be in store for him and his Scouts.

By 09:30, the jeep was packed, and they were headed back up Highway 538 for two reasons; the first, the contents of the cargo, and the second, Latoure was familiar with that route back to Da Nang. Not much was said between the two; both were concentrating more on the area around the jeep as it moved north toward Da Nang. On hindsight, being what it was, Latoure had wished he had asked for a radio so they could call for assistance if needed. Luckily, it wasn't, but he placed that bit of knowledge in his mind for use at a later time if necessary.

They arrived at the Division a little before noon. Latoure helped Hardy carry the locked cargo into the G-2, wishing there would have been a dolly nearby to use; of course, there was not. Everybody who was somebody were waiting inside for their arrival. Latoure finally began to grasp the importance of what he was to be involved with. Hardy told the powers that be that Latoure was already briefed on the use and deployment of the sensors and recommended that Latoure be allowed to return to the First Marines. There was a lot more going on which was way above Latoure's pay grade, and he was dismissed.

With his intel satchel in hand, he drove down Highway 1; his mind was swimming in information and the need for more information.

The Captain was waiting for him and told Latoure he knew most of what was going on, but his team was once again needed. This time a Marine A-4 Aircraft was endanger of crashing, so the pilot had to jettison both bomb racks, putting a dozen 250-pound bombs in the hand of the enemy to use as booby traps in the highways in and around Da Nang. Latoure followed the Intelligence Officer in the S-2 and over to the map. The pilot reported to within one thousand meters where the bomb racks impacted the place called Charlie Ridge, right smack dab in VC country. The plan was to put his team in the rear of a six-by-six truck heading south in a convoy to Seventh Marine unit on Hill 37. The driver would slow so the team could jump off. The key word here was slow, not stop. Once again, his only reply could have been and was, "Aye, aye, sir. Will do." The team was scheduled to depart at 04:30, so it would still be dark when they leaped from the truck. Of course, the Scouts were waiting for Latoure; each one with a variation of a shit-eating grin. They lived for action such as this.

Latoure talked with the six-by-six driver whose nickname was Snowball, and it fit him perfectly. He had red cheeks and a plump face a Santa would want to be. He was a pleasant enough Marine, and Latoure thought there was something else to Snowball than met the eye. The team took up positions in the rear of the truck, laying on the bed rather than the wooden seats so anyone looking in the back would see only cargo. As they approached the drop-off point, Snowball called back two minutes max. The Scouts tightened up their web gear, preparing for the jump into the jungle.

The engine of the truck raced; then Snowball reduced a gear. The truck lurched, and it was time. One by one, the Scouts eased over the rear tailgate, placing their left foot in the rear step, then making the leap of faith into the darkness. Latoure heard the truck once again shift back into a higher gear and sped down toward Hill 37. There was a ditch about five yards from the road where the team met. No injuries, no problems; then Can took point up Charlie Ridge. The team felt it would be easy to find the bomb rack, thinking they would have plowed up the jungle, leading the way to the bombs. If more than twenty-four hours had passed, the jungle would have reclaimed the path; however, it was just a little more than twenty-four hours.

When anyone looked at Charlie Ridge from Highway 340, it appeared to be a gentle slope up to the crest of the ridge. The patrol soon found out that it wasn't the case. Ascending, they came across ravine after ravine, and at the bottom of the ravine were footprints. The farther up they went, there were more footprints; the last revealed more than one hundred sets. This was definitely VC country. Can raised a fist, stopping the patrol, and he pointed to his ear. All members strained their hearing and heard the voices of the enemy and the banging of metal. They crept forward another thirty or so yards, and there was a group of ten Viet Congs working to free up one of the 250-pound bombs. The VC had fashioned a pole with a hook; four of them lifted the bomb and headed down Charlie Ridge off to the patrol's right. Latoure pointed at Kirby and Tang then made a throat-cutting motion, pointing at the group of four VCs. He added a trigger-pulling motion, meaning they could engage with weapon fire. Off the two Scouts went, in pursuit of the enemy and the bomb.

The remaining patrol members slowly moved into a position to engage the remaining six VCs. Latoure told them to wait until Kirby and Tang opened fire before they fired upon the enemy. All nodded, verifying the order. Time seemed to stand still for the next few minutes, then the M16 fire of Kirby and Tang echoed in the morning air. It was over almost before it began; Latoure and his fellow patrol members made short work of the six VCs. The enemy had done the Scouts a favor by moving both bomb racks within four feet of each other. Latoure made quick work of using the C-4 explosive satchel priming the blocks and placing them where they would ignite the 250-pound ordnance. Learning his lesson from his previous experience with the C-4 on Pipestone, this time all bombs had double-primed C-4 set to blow them up. He told the remaining three to take off toward Kirby and Tang and wait for him there. Quietly, they made their way through the jungle. Latoure knew that the remaining eleven bombs would shake the earth and leave a huge crater, so he gave the patrol five full minutes before setting off the fuse and took off running. Five minutes of time fuse was what Latoure had used, hoping it would be enough time for him to be out of the blast radius.

The ground beneath his feet lifted then settled back down, followed by dirt, rocks, trees and metal from the bomb racks. Latoure thought maybe a ten-minute fuse might have been better as he lay prone behind a huge rock. When the sky stopped falling, he stood and took off in the direction of the rest of the patrol. Kirby and Tang had moved the VC bodies, hiding them in the jungle, never to be found. The four members of the patrol lay in a circle around the remaining 250-pound bomb. Latoure had what was referred to as a mouse-trap detonator and thought, *Why not leave Charlie a present.* (Vietcongs were sometime called Charlie.) With both Tang and Can's help, they disguised the booby trap under the bomb and got in patrol order, moving downslope back toward Highway 340.

Can once again was point man; Latoure was next, followed by Brownie's replacement—a kid called Red, from the backwoods of West Virginia. Red wasn't a newbie; he had been wounded, treated, and released. Latoure's Intel Scouts were getting a reputation throughout the Division, and Red wanted in. Behind Red was Kirby and Tang, walking tail end Charlie—a very important place, which ensured the enemy didn't sneak up on the rear of the patrol. Can began waving his hand back and forth, meaning "Get off the trail ASAP." The explosion had sent a signal to every VC unit in and around Charlie Ridge that a ten-man unit was headed toward them. The patrol's choices were simple: fight or flight. To prevent this particular enemy unit from impeding the patrol's progress off Charlie Ridge, they engaged them with a fierce field of fire, dropping them in their tracks. Normally, bodies would be searched for Intel, but Latoure felt it was more prudent to didi off the ridge.

Kirby had twisted his ankle as he dived off the trail, so Red moved to his side, offering his shoulder so Kirby could keep some weight off his ankle. This made it even more important to get farther down and completely off the ridge. This patrol, Latoure was humping the radio, and the Command was screaming into the handset, wanting to know what was going on. Latoure only said one word, "Contact!" which shut up the Command.

They hadn't traveled much more than ten minutes when, to the rear of the patrol, rounds began soaring over their heads. Both Tang and Can were kneeling side by side, returning the VC fire.

Latoure told Red and Kirby, "Take off. We'll catch up."

The two Marines hustled down the trail; Kirby was hopping like the Easter Bunny. Latoure knelt between Can and Tang and pulled the LAAW from off his pack. Both Kit Carson Scouts shook their heads, acknowledging what Latoure was about to do. Latoure aimed at a huge tree about one hundred meters up the trail as rounds whistled by his ears and over his head. When the round impacted the tree, the explosion sent tree and dirt into the air. All three jumped up and began running down the trail, hoping to get off the ridge sooner rather than later. The jungle was thinning out rapidly, so they knew they were close to Highway 340. As they broke the tree line, Red and Kirby had taken up a blocking position on the east side of the road. They joined them, fanning out and ready to engage any enemy who came out of the jungle.

Someone at the Command figured the Patrol was in deep kimchee and dispatched a Platoon from Mike Company, Third Battalion, First Marines. Latoure heard their radio call and let the Platoon know where the Scouts were hiding. The Platoon was running toward the Patrol down the middle of Highway 430; Latoure radioed that wasn't a good idea as Charlie Ridge was a hornet's nest of pissed off VCs. The Lieutenant acknowledged and moved his unit into the same ditch where the Scouts were hiding. The Lieutenant's unit took up a blocking position with weapons aimed at the jungle across the highway.

He turned to Latoure and said, "That was you guys who blew the top of Charlie Ridge away?" Latoure nodded as the Lieutenant continues, "I'll be damned. You guys are something."

The initial plan was a deuce and half would pick the patrol up when radioed. Latoure made the call and was assured the vehicle was on its way from Hill 37, just to the south. A few Viet Congs dared to break the tree line but were quickly met with fire from the Lieutenant's Platoon. Latoure told the Lieutenant that there was at least a Battalion-sized VC unit in the jungle of Charlie Ridge. With that information and no approval from the Command, his Platoon waited until the vehicle arrived, picking up the Scouts to return them back to base. Latoure thanked the Lieutenant and his Platoon for the backup then climbed into the truck cab. Kirby had his ankle taped at the Regimental Aid Station; the rest of the Scouts cleaned their weapons and gear before going to noon chow. Latoure's responsibility was to debrief the patrol at the Command Center. The Regimental Commander and Lieutenant Colonel Vreeland listened intently to his debrief. He apologized for not searching the bodies but added that five against a battalion was just a little outside his Scouts' ability.

Both of the Officers laughed and told him, "Job well done as usual." He was dismissed and had a destination in mind, which wasn't the Intel Hut.

He exited the Command Bunker and moved across the compound, heading for the S-1 and Staff Sergeant Stone. When he entered, Admin Staff Sergeant Stone said, "I heard you were in it again, Sergeant Latoure."

"That was an understatement," Latoure answered.

"Bad news, buddy. Only three quotas for Hong Kong this month. Sorry. You were fourth on the list. You can wait to see if any of the other three cancel if you want?"

"Shit" was the only reply Latoure could muster.

"Listen, pal, I have this quota for Tokyo for the past two months, almost three. It's yours if you want it."

Then the Staff Sergeant handed Latoure a book whose title was *Tokyo After Dark*. He had already read and reread *Hong Kong After Dark* a half dozen times. They were novels about a spy; however, the author used actual places and, in some cases, people in those cities.

"When do I have to let you know, Staff Sergeant Stone?" he inquired.

"The R&R is in three days," Stone answered.

"Let me think about it. I will let you know?" he said.

"No problem. Go get a shower and some sleep," Stone replied.

He stopped by the S-2 and asked the Captain if it would be okay for him to go to Tokyo instead of Hong Kong. The Captain knew the command was piling on a lot of duties for Latoure and gave him his approval. He walked over to the field phone, cranked the handle, asked for S-1, and said, "Put me in for Tokyo, please."

CHAPTER 6

Rest and Recuperation: Tokyo After Dark

Latoure read, reread, and reread again the novel about the super spy who was in and around the Far East. *Tokyo After Dark, Hong Kong After Dark, Bangkok After Dark*, and *Manila After Dark* were passed among the Marines who dreamed of R&R in those exotic places. They were more sex novel than a travel guide, but the places described seemed real enough. Hotels, restaurants, clubs, dance halls, strip clubs, and wild women were described in graphic detail. There were two places of interest in and around Tokyo. First was the Perfect Room Hotel, managed by Johnny Matsunada, who, according to the author, could get anything for the book's number one spy, Rod Damian. The second was Roppongi, the most foreign-friendly area in and around Tokyo. Latoure thought the book was pure fiction; however, it did contain many details of people, places, and things. Along with the information in the novel, Latoure read what the intelligence community called pointy-talkies, which outlined relevant phrases of the languages in different countries. He hoped those outlined in the Japanese pointy-talky would come in handy during his stay in Japan. Dressed in his Charlie uniform of short-sleeved shirt and dress trousers; because the October temperature was still in the hundreds, a long-sleeved shirt with tie would be a walking sauna. He stopped by the Scouts' side of the hut and told them to take care. He would see them soon.

Ski gave him a lift to Da Nang Airfield R&R Center, where Latoure presented his travel orders to the clerk who informed him that the flight would be leaving in about ninety minutes and to go to waiting area Bravo. The only other enlisted waiting on the flight was an Army Specialist 4. A Spec 4 was an equivalent rank to a Corporal in the Marines. The remaining waiting area was full of brass from all branches of the US Military. Not the lower ranks of Lieutenants or Captains, but field-grade officers—Majors, Lieutenant Colonels, and higher—more than likely going to what was referred to as a Boon Daggle rather than official duties, which gave them a chance to get out of Vietnam for a couple days usually under the guise of a conference.

Latoure sat down next to the specialist and introduced himself; and Specialist Scully told him that he was going on R&R as well. Latoure asked him if he had read *Tokyo After Dark*; he hadn't. Latoure pulled it out of his ditty bag and said, "Read the pages I have tagged. You might find it interesting."

The specialist flipped through the pages while they both waited to board. After about thirty minutes, the Army man said, "Boy, wouldn't it be great if what was in here was true."

To which, Latoure readily agreed.

Boarding began by rank, of course, meaning the two enlisted men were last to board. It was so hot walking to the aircraft; Latoure thought an egg would fry on the cement. He has heard later in his career that some actually tried to do just that and were successful. The crew had saved the seats at the emergency exit for the two enlisted men; the aircrew knew that the enlisted were the best choice to open the emergency exit and help others out. There were a couple of pretty stewardesses, but with all the brass on the aircraft, he or Scully had a snowball's chance in hell of getting a date with them, so he leaned back for the two-hour flight and closed his eyes.

The landing woke him up, and as required, the two waited until all the officers left the aircraft. Latoure thanked the stewardess as he passed her exiting the plane down the stairs. At the bottom waited an Air Force person handing Field Jackets to all as they deplaned. Latoure waved him off and continued walking toward the terminal. He hadn't walked ten steps when the cold hit him like a brick wall. One-hundred-plus temperatures in Da Nang didn't prepared him for the twenty degrees at Tokyo. The specialist followed Latoure's lead, who also in short sleeves.

He looked at him and remarked, "Boy, you Marines are rock-hard."

Latoure laughed but picked up the pace to get inside the terminal as fast as he could without bringing attention to either of them.

Latoure scanned the area once inside the terminal, which mainly meant all the beautiful women walking throughout. Specialist Scully tapped him on the shoulder, pointing to the area clearly marked R&R Check-in. Latoure thought it was a good thing he had made friends with Scully or he might have walked right past it while looking at the women. They walked up to the counter and presented their orders. The Admin Clerk was very helpful in explaining what would be expected of them during their stay in Tokyo. Behind the clerk was an extremely large bulletin board; the kind where you pushed white letters in slots to spell out whatever the announcement was. On this board was a list of all the approved R&R-friendly hotels within Tokyo. The clerk explained they would have to pay him for the hotels at the counter, which would prevent the hotel from cheating or price gouging. Believe it or not, the last hotel available on the board was The Perfect Room.

"Did you read the part about the hotel?" Latoure asked Scully.

He replied, "No."

"That's the hotel in the book. The last one." Latoure told the clerk, "The Perfect Room please."

The clerk picked up the phone and dialed a number. Both of them understood immediately why this clerk was manning the desk because he began speaking in perfect Japanese, ending the conversation with "Hai, Domo!"

"You guys are all set. Go grab a taxi and watch out for the door of the cab. It opens automatically."

They both thanked the clerk and headed for the taxi stand.

The cabs were all lined up in a military fashion, one behind the other; as they approached the first one in line, the door flew open. Both slid inside, and Latoure, trying his best to speak Japanese, told the driver, "Perfect Room Hotel, *dozo*."

The driver began shaking his head like he didn't know where it was. Latoure pulled out the hotel receipt and pointed to the address listed on it. The driver then began shaking his head up and down, and off they went. The driver could have driven the two of them around the city and ran up the bill, but that was not the Japanese way. They had both exchanged some of their US Dollars for Japanese Yen at the R&R Counter and paid the driver with a little extra upon their arrival at The Perfect Room. It was a medium-sized building and very clean on the outside; it was rising up from the street for around ten stories. When they entered, all the staff bowed and said, "Irasshai matsu." Meaning "Welcome to the hotel."

The Manager was wearing a huge smile and waited behind the desk. His name tag read "Matsunada." *Things are getting really strange,* Latoure thought to himself, approaching the desk. Matsunada-san knew that they were coming, having received the call from the R&R Center. However, he was not prepared for what Latoure asked next.

"Excuse me, is your name or nickname Johnny?"

"How is you know that?" the Manager replied with a puzzled look.

"You are famous, Matsunada-san. Your name is in my book, saying you can do or make anything happen in Tokyo." Latoure reached in his ditty bag and pointed out Johnny's name and the Perfect Room pages in the book. "You may keep the book, Matsunada-san."

"Johnny, please." Which both Latoure and Scully acknowledge with a nod. He continued, "Please tell me what you like to drink, what kinds of food you like to eat, and what kind of *Josei-chan* you prefer."

Latoure let Scully go first then told Johnny, "Rum and coke, hamburgers, and red hair. But I know that this is Japan, so black hair is fine."

"Please go into the Lounge. It is closed except for my special guests, as you both are."

They walked into the lounge and sat at the bar, where Johnny mixed them both drinks. "I will have some lunch fixed for you while I prepare your rooms, okay?"

"Johnny, don't do anything special just for us. We are no one special," Latoure told Johnny, which Scully agreed with. That statement was conveniently ignored. Johnny's command of the English language was outstanding; Latoure choosing this hotel was right on point.

Less than ten minutes later, a Chef came and gave them hand-formed burgers, which included a basket made of julienne potatoes filled with bright green peas. The burger was outstanding, and the rum and coke only added to its flavor. Johnny came back into the lounge to check on them and prepared a second round of drinks before rushing off again. What they didn't know was that the hotel had two suites on the eleventh or top floor. One of the suites was occupied, but Johnny made them move down to the tenth floor so each of his new friends could have a private suite on the same floor. He also made a phone call to a friend with a shady past known in the yakuza. Satisfied all would be ready soon, he joined the two guests in the lounge with the book in hand. Time seemed to fly by as Johnny pointed out in the book that this was a good place or that wasn't a good place, almost page by page.

The phone behind the bar rang; Johnny excused himself and answered it. He seemed very pleased after hanging up and came back sitting between Latoure and Scully, this time sharing a drink with them. Scotch was his drink of choice. "Your rooms are almost ready. Less than five minutes more," Johnny told them. "I will be right back please to wait." Less than a minute passed when Johnny returned. He gave Latoure a key stamped with 1102 and another stamped with 1101 to Scully. "Please finish your drinks. I took the liberty to have the Bell Captain take your bags to your rooms." They tried to pay for lunch and their drinks, but Johnny would not accept any money.

During the elevator ride to the eleventh floor, Scully told Latoure that he was sure glad they met, and he was looking forward to the rest of their R&R. They agreed to get together around 20:00 to go out and see what the city had in store for them. Upon opening the door to his room, Latoure heard water running. Not more than two or three steps inside, a tray was set and on it, a bottle of Bacardi, a six-pack of Pepsi, plus a bucket of ice. Off to his left, there were tatami mats with a Japanese table in the middle, much like on Okinawa. To his right was an extremely large bed with so many pillows the entire Intel Scouts could have had one. Straight back in the direction of where the water sounds came from, behind a partially closed door, Latoure figured it was from the bathroom and went to investigate.

Leaning over a large tub and filling it was a girl with auburn hair. Latoure startled her as much as he did himself. "Go men," he said, thinking she was housekeeping, and the room wasn't ready yet.

She walked over to him, offered her hand, and said, "Yuriko, your companion."

Now, totally confused, he said, "Yuriko-san, my pleasure. What do you mean by 'your companion?'"

"Johnny-san has arranged for me to escort you around Tokyo during your stay. If you do not like me, he will also find another." Yuriko was not as beautiful as Michiko, but she was pretty in her own special way. Johnny had done his best to find a redhead for him, and Latoure was not about to be ungrateful. She added, "I am here for your pleasure."

"What will I owe you, Yuriko-san?" he asked.

"Nothing. My services have been compensated for," she replied.

"Are you happy knowing you must stay with me, Yuriko-chan?" He changed her name to the less formal *chan* rather than *san*.

"Very happy. You are a handsome man. I think maybe Paul Newman, yes."

He laughed. Her English was very good, and rather than hang out with Scully, Yuriko was much prettier. "My name is Larry. Please call me that, Yuriko-chan." *L*s and *R*s were letters that the Japanese had problems pronouncing, but she tried her best.

She had prepared a bath for him; just like in Okinawa, the small stool was ready for him. She was wearing a kimono-type robe, which she removed. Latoure had problems keeping his eyeballs in his head. Her body seemed to be carved from porcelain.

"Dozo, Larry-san." She was pointing at his uniform. He knew enough to remove his shoes before entering the suite, but the steam from the bath wasn't doing his uniform any good. He grabbed a robe from a peg along the wall and moved back into the main part of the room. She followed him, and as he removed a piece of his clothes, she shook it out, then hung it neatly in the closet. He left his boxers on but put the robe over the top of his seminude body.

Returning to the bath, Yuriko wasted no time removing his robe, and as she knelt, she deftly slipped down his boxers as she pointed to the stool. Having had the pleasure of a Japanese bath before, Latoure kind of knew what to expect. She took the plastic size wash pan, filled it from the bath, and poured it over his head. If there was a word to describe hot other than "hot," he would have used it. Damn, that water was steaming, but he began to immediately feel better as she took the oversize sponge, soaping him down from head to foot. Rinsing him off, he asked, "Again please, Yuriko-chan. I haven't been able to wash very good in Vietnam."

Once again, she soaped him from head to foot. She steadied him as he tried to lift his leg over the edge of the tub, which was over four feet high. It was very hot, but she gave him no choice once his right leg was in the tub; she gave him a shove, and his body followed. Soon, he was neck-deep in the hot water and leaned back, allowing it to relax his muscles. She cleaned up the bath area but did not join him in the tub. It wasn't long before he understood why she didn't. His pores were opened wide by the hot water, and six months of dirt and grime began to float on the surface. It seemed even the shower he had built didn't help to clean him. There was at least one-quarter inch of dirt floating on the surface. She told him to get out of tub so she could drain it. Then without missing a beat, began to give him another sponge bath while the tub refilled. His skin was beet red by the time she finished his second scrubbing. His second time entering the tub wasn't as bad as the first, now knowing what to expect with the hot water. What he didn't expect was Yuriko removing the rest of her clothes and joining him in the tub.

The phone began to ring; he hustled out of the tub, answering it. Johnny asked him if everything was to his satisfaction and was there anything more he could do before leaving for the evening. Latoure asked how he can compensate Matsunada for all he has done for them; to which, Johnny said that everything was paid for by the R&R Center. Latoure knew that wasn't true but didn't press the issue.

He thanked Johnny once more before hanging up. Checking the time, he noticed it was almost 19:30 or 7:30 p.m. for civilians. He went back into the bath, still nude, and told Yuriko that they were going out at eight with Scully. What Latoure didn't know was Scully received the same treatment as he just did, with another pretty girl.

"Where we go, Larry-san?" she asked.

"You pick, Yuriko. Dinner, drink, and dancing okay?" he answered.

"Hai so desu," she replied.

Latoure put on the clothes he wore the night on Okinawa where the four of them went out but didn't have a coat of any type to keep him warm on the streets of Tokyo. She asked if he had a coat and, upon hearing his answer, picked up the phone, calling the front desk. Five minutes later, a sport coat was dropped off at the room. He called Scully, who told Latoure he had died and had gone to heaven. Latoure told him he knew the feeling. They added thirty minutes to allow the girls time to put on their makeup. Yuriko had brought a small bag with change of clothes in it, but Latoure knew that there wasn't enough to last for his full R&R. He reached into the hidden pocket of his ditty bag, counting out $1,000 and putting the remainder back. He figured one hundred dollars a day should cover all their expenses. He walked over to Yuriko and handed the thousand dollars to her.

"I trust you, Yuriko-chan. This should be enough for us and anything left over is special for you."

He had little fear that she would cheat him, especially knowing that he was connected to Johnny Matsunada in some form or fashion. He could see a definite change in Yuriko's demeanor. Yes, she was pleasant enough initially, but now a glow seemed to ruminate from her. She had brought a midthigh cocktail dress in a navy blue, which hugged her body in all the right places, plus heels.

"We go eat, then maybe dance or listen music tonight. This okay, Larry-san?" Yuri asked.

"Sounds wonderful, Yuriko. I just realized I am really hungry." It dawned on him that less than twenty-four hours earlier, he was in the middle of a combat zone and was now with a pretty woman, getting ready to paint the town. Part of him wished that one of his Scouts could have been there enjoying this as well.

Scully answered the door with an ear-to-ear shit-eating grin, which told Latoure all he needed to know about what Scully had been doing. In this case, his duties as an intelligence analyst gave him too much information, especially about the sexually transmitted diseases in the Far East; and unlike his time with Michiko, this time, he would be responsible. The issue at hand was where to get what would be needed later that night and for the rest of his stay in Tokyo.

During the elevator ride, Latoure spent a little too much time soaking in Scully's date, whose name was Yumiko. It was too much of a coincidence that the girls' names were Yuriko and Yumiko; most likely these were not their real names.

Yuriko grabbed his arm, bringing him out of his daze, asking, "You want maybe some other girl, Larry-san?" she asked.

"*Go men,* Yuri-chan. I was thinking about my job and my men. You make me very happy." Saying that appeased her, and off they went. He thought he heard Yuri say, "Ginza Rengatai, dozo," to the taxi driver and sat back, saying, "*Mousugu.* Very soon!"

The Rengatai was a Japanese restaurant that specialized in American food. Steaks, omelets, pasta, and all sorts of familiar dishes. Yumiko was not that familiar with American foods, but she read it item by item before finally settling on spaghetti. It was a huge hamburger steak with fried potatoes for Latoure and Scully, while Yuriko only asked for a club sandwich. The food was actually very tasty and was served very quickly. Latoure whispered to Yuriko, "We pay for all, okay?"

She nodded. "Yes."

After dinner, they walked a couple blocks on the streets of Ginza with the girls pointing out places of interest or places where they should or would not go. They turned down a very narrow alley that was lit up as bright as the Vegas strip. Halfway down the alley, music could be heard as jazz club was their destination, but the band played more swing-type music than jazz. Yuriko definitely was in charge. The Doorman tried to discourage the group from entering, but whatever she told him changed his demeanor quick. They were seated in a raised section that provided them an excellent view of the five-piece band and very close to a small dance floor. Relying on his Okinawa jazz club experience, he ordered a bottle of Suntory whiskey for the table.

He looked at Scully and said, "When in Rome!" Yuriko was smiling ear to ear that he knew what to do.

Suntory mixed with bottled water flowed like the river over Niagara Falls. Taking advantage of the dance lessons he learned as a kid, he and Yuriko became the center of attraction by all guests and staff at the club; many of the guests were applauding their efforts. The girls took a bathroom break, which gave the men time to compare notes. Of course, Scully, with an inflated chest, told him about his lovemaking prowess, and Latoure asked if he gave the gift of love.

Scully replied, "What the hell are you talking about, Jarhead?" If looks could kill, Latoure's stare let Scully know he had crossed the line. "Sorry, Sarge, too much booze."

"That's okay. Don't let it happen again. Now, did you use a rubber?"

"Yumiko had a couple but no more."

"Then let's find a drugstore on the way back."

It was almost 2:00 a.m. when they left the Jazz Club. Latoure stopped Yuriko a short way up the alley. He had the pointy-talky in his back pocket and found what he needed to know. "Doku Kusuriya, Yuri-chan?"

She wasn't quite sure what he was asking, so he pointed to the phrase, asking for directions to a drug store. "You sick, Larry-san?" she asked.

Shaking his head and smiling ear to ear, he told her, "No." A few seconds later, the light went on, and she returned his smile with one of her own.

Back on the street, she looked left and right, then pointed up the street to the right. Off the group went. When they arrived at the drug store, Yuriko put her hand in Latoure's chest and said, "You wait, *dozo*."

So they stood, looking at their surroundings. Across the street, it looked like many people were playing slot machines, and the noise emanating from there was very loud. Every time the door opened, the sound of crashing metal balls was heard. The girls came out, each carrying a small bag.

"You ready, Larry-san?"

He told her, "Yes." Then he pointed across the street, asking, "What's that place?"

"Pachinko," she told him.

He thought he might like to visit one during his stay in Tokyo. They flagged down a taxi, where Scully forgot about the automatic doors as it smashed into him. Latoure caught him before he fell to the ground, and all began laughing aloud, even the taxi driver joined in.

The ride back to the hotel seemed over before it began; they poured out of the cab rather than stepping out. All were a little weary from that night's activity. Scully and Yumiko were all over each other on the street, in the lobby, and on the elevator. Latoure had read public display of affection were frowned upon in Japan, so he took the gentleman's approach. Once the door to the room closed behind them, all bets were off; he took Yuriko in his arms and kissed her passionately. She was surprised but returned his passion with her own, twofold.

"Shower, Larry-san?"

"Hai," he replied.

They did not use the small stool; they were standing face-to-face, lathering each other from head to foot. As she rinsed the soap from him, he thought he needed to make amends for his staring at Yumiko earlier and show her that she was more than enough woman for him. The question was, Would the six months of forced celibacy have an effect on his lovemaking? He rinsed the lather from Yumiko, and as they dried one another off, she said, "Larry-san, I leave in morning to go to Genkou (bank) to change your money to Japanese yen. We will have tons of money then to have fun. Plus I pick up more clothes from my *ouchi*. Maybe three or four hours, *dozo?*"

He shook his head yes as he picked her up and carried her into the bedroom.

He laid her gently in the middle of the mattress. His butterfly kisses began at her hairline, slowly moving from left to right, then lowering his mouth an inch or so; he began to kiss her across her eyebrows. He made a complete circle around her left ear before leaving another trail of kisses across her cheek, over her nose, then with more butterfly kisses, circled her right ear. Now slowly to her lips, he wanted to leave a hundred kisses over her top lip and a hundred more on her bottom lip. She tried vainly to kiss him back, but he moved his mouth down her chin and kissed her neck once again from left side to right.

He read in the *After Dark* novel that the nape of the neck was an erotic zone for Japanese women; as he continued to kiss her neck, he gently turned her onto her stomach. Yuriko emitted a sigh as her body seemed to melt into the bed while he kissed the back of her neck. He left a trail of butterfly kisses down the outside of her arm to her palm and then kissed each finger. Then back up the inside of her arm and over her shoulders, where he gave her left arm the same. He went back up to the middle of her back and down her spine. She tried to turn back over, but Latoure was too strong and told her to "Relax and enjoy, *dozo*!"

After leaving kisses all over her back, he gently turned her over so he could continue to caress and kiss the front of her body. Starting at the collarbone then down one side of her body but avoiding the center of her; he went back up to the other collarbone and back down. Her body trembled as he kissed and licked closer and closer to her center. She began having her first orgasm within moments as he licked the center of her being. Her legs trembled as he reached for the package she placed on the nightstand. He kept kissing her and caressing her to keep her desire and passion soaring. She sighed as he entered her so very slowly. Only halfway and slowly for a few moments, then quickly, before filling her fully; slowly at first then rapid thrusts. Over and over again, he went shallow, slow, then fast; then deep, slow, and fast. He thought of baseball, combat patrols, and Okinawa as he tried to fill his mind, knowing he wouldn't last very long, wanting to pleasure Yuriko completely.

Her back arched, lifting him high into the air as he pulsed with his release. Her body became limp with no movement at all, which concerned him. He placed his ear first close to her mouth to see if she was still breathing and his hand on her heart to feel it beating. Thankfully, she was in both, shallow as it was. He rolled onto his back to sleep, exhausted from the day and night's pleasurable activities. Within seconds, he was lost in a deep sleep.

He never felt Yuriko as she quietly rose from the bed. She stared at her lover as she dressed then picked up her small bag. A smile crossed her face while she slipped silently from the suite. She knew she had to return with his dollars exchanged to yen or perhaps give it to Matsunada-san. She missed her four-year-old daughter, who was being kept by her mother while she tried to eke a living for all three of them. Her father had passed earlier that year, and with no other family, it was up to her. She walked to the bus stop, intending to exchange the dollars first, then her daughter.

Latoure awoke with his mind in a fog, not sure of his surroundings. As his brain cleared, he turned on his side; Yuriko was not there. He checked the rest of the suite for her before he recalled her telling him about going to the bank. The next order of business was to complete the daily S's—shit, shower, and shave—but before that, he called the desk and ordered a large pot of coffee. Some time as he was completing his early morning tasks, the staff had slipped inside and placed the coffee on the table. As he stepped from the bathroom, the smell of the coffee filled his senses; and still wrapped in a towel, he drank two full cups before dressing.

He knocked on Scully's door, but there was no answer. He rode the elevator down; this time, food was on his mind. Johnny saw him step from the elevator and called him over, handing Latoure an envelope. As he opened the envelope, Johnny asked if everything was okay. Latoure told him that he was very pleased with his stay and was looking forward to seeing the rest of Tokyo. He heard Scully and Yumiko laughing in the restaurant and took two steps in that direction. The envelope was filled with yen, and he turned back to Johnny, asking, "Where's Yuriko-san?"

Johnny told Latoure that she thought you were not pleased with her and told me to find another girl for you.

"Can you get Yuriko-san to come back? I think there is a huge misunderstanding, Matsunada-san."

Johnny told him, "I will try my best."

"Please try hard and thank you."

He joined Scully and Yumiko at their table, telling them about Yuriko. Yumiko, shaking her head, said, "I know she was missing her daughter, and today was her birthday."

That statement made Latoure feel even more like an ass. "She thinks I am not pleased with her, Yumiko-san. That isn't true one bit."

Their food arrived, and suddenly, Latoure wasn't that hungry. Excusing himself, he left and rode the elevator back to his room. He plopped down on the bed and began thinking on how he could make amends for what he did. *I sure can screw things up,* he thought, just before falling asleep again.

About an hour later, the phone rang, and Johnny began to apologize to him for Yuriko-san's absence. Latoure assured Johnny that it was all his fault and not Yuriko's. Johnny further told him that Yuriko-san would return tomorrow morning if that was okay. Of course, it would be, since he now knew that it was her daughter's birthday, and told Johnny this. Then he asked if it would be okay to talk face-to-face, rather than on the phone, if he had some time for him. Johnny told him, "Of course, it would be."

He splashed some water on his face and headed back down to the front desk.

Johnny wasn't at the front desk. A really beautiful woman was there. As he approached the desk, she just smiled and pointed toward the lounge. Latoure acknowledge with a nod and a smile and went in to join Johnny, who already had mixed drinks for them.

"I see you have met my daughter, Latoure-san," Johnny said.

"That is your daughter on the front desk?" Latoure replied. Which was confirmed with a nod of his head. "She is very beautiful, Matsunada-san." Again, a reply with a nod of the head. "I really messed up last night, Matsunada-san. I kept staring at Yumiko too much, so Yuriko felt I didn't like her. I need to make it up to her, so I thought I would get a gift for her and her daughter, but I do not know where to go."

"Ah, Latoure-san, that is very easy. Roppongi District is the most foreign-friendly place in Tokyo. I will write directions for the taxi."

"*Domo arigato,* Matsunada-san."

"Hai" was the reply with a shallow bow.

Their afternoon cocktails finished, both went their separate ways. Johnny went back to his office, and Latoure, out the front door, hailing a taxi and handing the driver the note with directions to Roppongi. It didn't seem that far from the hotel and also looked a little familiar to him as he stepped from the cab. Even in the afternoon, the district was lit up like the Vegas strip. Signs in both Japanese and English directed people to their respective destinations. Johnny had told him there was a huge shopping area, and after asking three different people, he finally found his intended destination.

He entered the Takashimaya Department Store, a huge building with around ten floors or so. Two young women bowed and welcomed him. He asked where he could find a doll, which they didn't understand, but through sign language and motions, they understood what he was looking for. The fifth floor was where he was directed toward; the elevator ride was filled with relaxing music, and it stopped at his floor very quickly. The previous year was the Year of the Monkey, so there was a myriad of different toy monkeys. Latoure settled on a sitting monkey with cymbals in both hands; turn the key and it would bounce while playing them. He also picked up a Red-Haired Raggedy Ann Doll.

Then it was time to give himself a present. He couldn't very well wear the same clothes he bought on Okinawa for the entire R&R, so he purchased two pairs of trousers, two polo shirts, and a windbreaker. He felt his black dress socks would do the trick. On his way out of the Department Store, he passed a jewelry counter displaying pearls. He couldn't resist a necklace with a single pearl for Yuriko-san.

As he walked down the street, shops filled the block on either side. A camera shop caught his eye. On display was a 110-capable camera, much like you would see in a spy film. He was tempted to go inside, but he wasn't sure at ¥15,000 what sort of bargain the camera was. He was also concerned if offering less than the sticker would be disrespecting the owner. In the Department Store, it was simple; what you saw on the ticket was what you paid, but he had read in the *Tokyo After Dark* novel that bargaining was expected at the small mom-and-pop stores.

As he continued walking down the street, he passed a Military Package Store. He did not expect a US Military Package Store in the middle of Tokyo, but there it was. When he went inside, there was a mixture of many nationalities. He had watched Johnny as he mixed drinks and knew that Johnnie Walker Scotch was Matsunada's drink of choice. He asked one of the salespeople what the difference was between the Red and Black Labels and was told the Black was the utmost. Because he was in more comfortable surroundings, he also asked about bargaining with the locals at their stores. He was told that it was an accepted practice. With that information, he returned up the street to the camera shop. After a few minutes of haggling with a very pleasant store owner, he purchased the camera for ¥12,000, plus the owner threw in three rolls of film.

He continued walking down the street and noticed the Playboy Bunny logo prominently displayed across the street. The road actually wasn't used that much by vehicle traffic, so with no problem, he crossed over to the Tokyo Playboy Club. Membership in the Playboy Club was way above his pay grade, but he would never get another chance like this, so he walked up the stairs to the front door, which opened automatically. The reason for the automatic door was because a Playboy Bunny had seen him cross the street and liked what she saw.

"Welcome to the Tokyo Playboy Club," the Anglo girl told him, all decked out in her bunny outfit, including the trademark cotton tail.

"I am not a member, but I couldn't resist. I really wanted to know how the other half lived," Latoure told her.

"We are very slow this time of day. Would you like a mini tour, soldier?"

"I am a Marine not a soldier, but if the invitation still stands, of course, I would like that tour."

"We don't get many Marines coming here on R&R. My brother is a Marine also." She offered her hand and told him, "My name is Jamie. That's my real name, not the one I use when I am a bunny, so please don't call me that. Missy will do once we are inside."

"Roger that, Missy."

He focused on the white cotton tail as Missy guided him through the first floor to the rear and pulled back a table so he could sit, looking at the entire room. "So what you are drinking, Jarhead."

Latoure laughed and said, "My name is Larry or Sergeant, whichever you prefer, Missy. Actually, a beer would be nice. Surprise me with whatever brand you think is good."

It was $7.50 for the beer so it would be one and done at the Playboy Club. As Missy sat down across from him, she told Latoure she would be off in about twenty or thirty minutes. She offered to show him around Roppongi if he were up to it. To say he was a little apprehensive would have been an understatement. His mind went to the buy-me-drink girls that Jones told him about.

"Are you serious, Missy?"

"Yes, I don't get to talk to an American, much less a Marine, that often." was her answer.

True to her word, twenty minutes later, she stopped by his table and said, "Meet me out front in five minutes please."

He nodded yes, and then the thought crossed his mind. *Who in the hell is watching over me?* He wished that he wasn't lugging around the shopping bag. It felt more like an anchor than a bag filled with clothes and gifts. Jamie walked up to him, dressed in blue jeans, a quilted coat, and gloves.

"Hungry?" she asked then inquired, "What's in the bag?"

"I bought some clothes plus scotch for the Manager and some trinkets for one of his employees for treating me so nice."

"That's great?" she said with a puzzled look.

To quell her curiosity, he explained, "He gave me one of the two suites. The other to an Army guy who is on R&R with me. Plus free booze, food, help, you name it. Johnny always comes through."

"What Hotel, Larry?"

"It's called the Perfect Room. I keep the R&R receipt to show taxi drivers because they don't even know where it is located."

"Let me see your receipt, please."

He handed it to her, and she said, "Oh, I know where you are staying now, not very far from here." Of course, Latoure knew that, having ridden a short distance in the taxi to Roppongi. "Let's find a noodle shop, okay?" she asked.

"Fine with me," he answered.

She ordered them both some sort of delicious bowl of noodles. As they ate, she told him she was a graduate student studying at the Tokyo University, hoping for a career in the Diplomatic Services. She was fluent in Japanese and could read it as well. The Club, as she called it, provided her with mad money because she was on a free ticket at the university. For the next twenty minutes, he learned just about everything that made up Jamie. She shared a room with another foreign student who happened to be on holiday at Mount Fuji. He tried hard not to read into what she was telling him. *But it didn't hurt to dream,* he thought.

As they left the Noodle Shop, Jamie slipped her hand around his arm. He felt it was nice.

"We need to swing by my apartment so I can change. That is if you want to go out with me tonight."

Of course, he did and told her so. She guided him beneath the street, to the trains, where he had his first train ride in Tokyo. She told him that using the trains was very easy, and it was almost impossible to get lost. Less than ten minute later, she almost yanked him off the train. He was a little mad until he saw how crazy the locals were getting both off and on the train. She told him the Japanese trains waited for no one and have a 99 percent on-time reputation. She was trying to keep him out of harm's way.

Three blocks from the underground station, she took them left for a few streets, then left again before stopping at a huge apartment building. The doorman opened the door and greeted them both as they entered. They took an elevator to the tenth floor then down the hallway to the last door on the left, which she unlocked and motioned him inside. They removed their shoes at the tiny alcove, entering the apartment. It wasn't that big; in fact his suite was much larger.

"Larry, I need to freshen up. What would you like to drink while you wait?"

"Beer's fine if you have it. If not, anything else as long as it is cold."

She set the Asahi Beer down and then went to the rear of the apartment, returning, wrapped in a large towel. "I will be back in a jiffy. The shower's down the hall." She scurried out the door. A few minutes later, she returned with towels around her head and body and smelling absolutely wonderful.

She stopped in front of him, placing her hands upon his knees and staring deeply into his eyes. As she was getting ready for her shower, she pulled out her futon bedding with hopes of what might happen. She leaned in and kissed him with a pent-up passion; then she took his hand and led him back him into her bedroom. They made love for hours on end, enjoying every inch of one another until both of them fell into a deep sleep. He woke up at 6:00 a.m., went into the kitchen, where he prepared them breakfast. She awoke while he was cooking and came up behind him, placing her arms around his waist and squeezing him tightly.

"I have to work at the Club then evening classes until 10:00 p.m."

"I understand you have to do you. Besides, I need to go back to my hotel as well."

"I want to see you again, Larry. How about Friday night for dinner and drinks?"

"That would be super, but I don't know how to find you here."

"I will come pick you up at the Perfect Room, okay?"

"Okay, just point me in the direction so I can find it today."

Jamie wrote a note in Japanese and English and said, "Follow these directions, and the train will drop you off a block from the Perfect Room. It will be about ¥500."

He kissed her deeply then told her, "See you Friday around five-ish, okay? And 1102 is my suite number."

"See you then," Jamie answered.

He left her place thinking, *Thank you. Thank you to whoever you are watching over me.*

It was around 9:30 a.m. when the train dropped him off. Jamie's directions were perfect. He stopped by the front desk and gave Johnny his present of the Johnnie Walker Black. Johnny's eyes widened, and he thanked him many times over for the scotch. Then he said that Yuriko-chan would come to see him around eleven o'clock. He thanked Johnny and rode the elevator to his room. It was time for his morning routine and a change of clothes. He was squeaky-clean. He tried on the clothes he bought. It was a perfect fit; the waist and length were correct, and the polo shirts didn't bind anywhere.

Johnny had sent up coffee; it was unasked for but much appreciated. As he sat there drinking a cup, he heard a soft knock on his door. Yuriko began bowing deeply over and over saying, "Gomen" over and over.

He took both her hands in his and gently pulled her inside his suite. Once the door closed, he took her in his arms and held her with affection. "How was your daughter's birthday, Yuriko-chan?" She stepped back with a puzzled looking on her face. "Yumiko-chan told me."

"We had a good time, Larry-san. Thank you for asking."

He then asked, "I didn't cause you any problems, did I?"

She didn't answer but only lowered her head. "Okay, I will fix it if I can." He took her hand and led her farther into the suite. She thought it would be in the direction of the bed, but he pulled a chair out and spoke, "*Dozo*. Coffee, Yuriko-chan, *disuka*."

She nodded as he began to pour her a cup. He then moved behind her, placing the pearl necklace around her neck. Tears formed in her eyes, and her heart warmed to this American.

"That is for mama-san, now for your daughter. What is her name please?" he asked.

"Junko," she told him.

"Well, this is for Junko-chan." He pulled the windup toy from the bag. He only did a couple turns of the key, but the monkey began playing its cymbals.

She laughed then said, "Junko will enjoy it."

"There is more, Yuriko, for her." He placed the Raggedy Ann doll in front of her. He was doing his best to right his wrongdoing to Yuriko. "Would it be okay if we took Junko out for a day of fun, Yuriko-chan?"

Shocked, she didn't answer right away, then she finally said, "Not today. She went with my Mother, shopping, but tomorrow if that is fine?"

"Of course," he answered. "So what shall we do today then, Yuriko?"

She stood and moved around the table, put her arms around him, then placed one of the most passionate kisses he ever felt upon his lips. Then she took his hand, leading him to the bed, for an hour of lovemaking.

They lay together; her head was upon his chest. "Shall we go out for dinner and dancing, just you and I?" he asked her.

"Of course, Larry-san, we can go anywhere you want." It wouldn't be for the next few hours, though, as she moved on top of him to seduce him once more. He willingly gave in to her. She was an extra special woman. She took time out to call her mother to tell her that she would be picking Junko up for a special time in the morning around 9:00 a.m. Of course, her mother wanted to know more, but Yuriko dodged her questions and said she had to go.

They didn't even try to see if Scully and Yumiko wanted to join them for dinner, drinks, and dancing. The two of them spent a wonderful evening, which included dinner at a traditional Japanese restaurant where he sampled something called shabu-shabu. A Japanese variant of the hot pot, consisting of thin slices of raw meat and fresh vegetables cooked in a pot of hot broth at the table. How could anyone complain about that special meal when they themselves picked what they wanted to eat, much like the Mongolian BBQ on Okinawa.

Yuriko took them to a different lounge with live music than the last time they went dancing. This place offered current music of the '60s and dances of that same era. The Stroll, Mashed Potatoes, Locomotion, Twist, plus a few Latoure wasn't familiar with. A smile never left Yuriko-chan that entire evening. The two of them spent so much time dancing, they hardly drank any liquor at all. She held his arm tightly, proud to be part of his life even if just for a few days.

Once back at the Perfect Room, they gave each other sponge baths, which involved more kissing and tickling than actual washing. He had no idea what time it was when they finally made it to the bedroom, nor did he know what time sleep finally came over them after a repeat performance of their lovemaking earlier in the day. Yuriko had surrender herself completely to her lover, no longer concerned that he didn't want to be with her. She looked at his chest that rose and fell in his deep sleep before finally letting sleep overcome her.

She woke around seven, called room service, and ordered a light breakfast and coffee for Larry-san. Then she washed and dressed before waking him up with a trail of kisses all over his face. She told him that she ordered food, and it was time for his lazy butt to get moving as she slapped it. As he went about his morning routine, he formed a plan to let Yuriko go either that day or early in the next morning, which would be Friday and his date with Jamie. Breakfast was already served by the time he finished and joined Yuriko at the small table. She asked if it would be okay to go to a place called KidZania with Junko today. She explained it was an adventure for kids where they got to experience what was required in different jobs. The children actually did the work; it was a hands-on place. Of course, he readily agreed. He dressed and then gave Yuriko the envelope containing the yen she had exchanged. He asked her what she would prefer, spending his last night with him tonight or with Junko after their outing. She, of course, said with him but thought he wasn't leaving until Saturday. He told her that she was correct, but he needed to do some things for his fellow Marines before leaving and needed to do it alone. It would not interest her, and he didn't think that Yakota Air Force Base would allow her to join him. She then understood and would decide what she wanted to do later.

Once again, he experienced the Japanese Train System crammed like sardines in the cars. He preferred to stand and did so as Yuriko sat in front of him. A short while later, they got off and walked toward Yuriko's house. She asked him to stop a few doors before her place. She didn't want her mother to create a scene when she saw Yuriko with an American. She had the bag with the toys inside and was still wearing the pearl necklace, walking to her family home. He stood waiting, and less than five minutes later, Yuriko came, walking toward him and holding the hand of a beautiful girl who was holding the doll he gave her in her dainty hand. She explained to Junko that Larry-san was a good friend and wanted to give her something special for her birthday and was the person who presented her with the doll.

The Japanese looked upon the three of them as they walked back to the train station. Some with smiles, others with indifference. Once again, true to form, the train was on time and not as packed as earlier in the day. When they arrived at their destination, Junko would walk between Yuriko and him but seemed afraid of Latoure. When they got to KidZania, Junko's face lit up with a smile from ear to ear. For the next three or four hours, Junko got to perform the duties of a nurse, dentist, and secretary. Each position required her to actually do the work. It was a hands-on experience. Yuriko would never have enough money for this type of luxury for Junko.

They went and ate a nice lunch, and Latoure felt Junko was even warming up to him. They were walking past a street vendor selling ice cream, and Latoure stopped them, asking, "Who wants ice cream?"

Junko understood that much and began jumping up and down. They sat together on a small bench; all three were licking their cones. As they ate their ice cream, Latoure turned to Yuriko and said, "I am sorry I couldn't do more, Yuriko. I also want to apologize for making you feel like I did not like or want you. This day, I will remember for a very long time."

A tear began forming in her eye as her daughter, totally oblivious to what they were talking about, attacked her ice cream. "Larry-san, you have brightened both me and my daughter's life with your kindness. I will keep a special place in my heart for you, and I will remind Junko of your kindness as well."

Tears were freely running down her cheeks. Using the napkin from the ice cream vendor, he dabbed at the tears. His stomach wrenched, but he knew that he would never return to Tokyo.

They stopped a few houses short of Yuriko and Junko's home. He told Yuriko that she had made his visit to Tokyo a beautiful experience. Then he asked what train would take him back to his hotel. He already knew and had the directions Jamie wrote for him.

"Stay with Junko. Just give me enough yen to get back to the hotel, *dozo*." He told her to keep what was left of the yen and leaned in and kissed her on her cheek. A sharp about-face, and he walked from her life forever.

He was getting very confident now riding the train system in and around Tokyo and found the stop for his hotel without any trouble. It was getting on toward dinnertime when he arrived, so he went into the lounge. The bartender seemed very familiar to him. Of course, it was Johnny's beautiful daughter. He asked where Johnny was, and she told him he took off for the rest of the day and asked if there was anything she might do for him. Her English was even better than Johnny's, so he asked her where she studied. She told Latoure that her father made them speak English only twice a week at their home, and she chose to study it as a major in college. They had just finished exams, so she was free for the next week or so. She liked it when she got to give her father a break from work, and now especially because he and Scully were there, she got to practice it.

He asked if it was okay to eat at the bar and to keep her company for a while; to which, she replied she would be happy if he would. Few customers passed in and out of the lounge, but for the majority of that Thursday evening, it was only the two of them. At one point, he asked her if he could know her name. She hesitated at first but then told him it was Hatsuko.

"What does Hatsuko mean, *dozo*?" Trying to impress her with his limited knowledge of Japanese.

"It means firstborn, and unfortunately I am their only child. My mother passed about five years ago, so my father threw himself into this hotel." It struck him as unusual that both Hatsuko and Junko were living almost the same life. One without a mother, the other without a father.

"You want to close, Hatsuko, so you can leave for home?" he asked her.

"I don't live at home. In fact, I live here as sort of a live-in manager."

His mind began working a mile a minute. Should he or shouldn't he? "Would you like my company or rather I head to my suite?"

"Please stay. I am enjoying our conversations. Besides, your friend is living in the suite I usually use."

"So you were the one Johnny made move so Scully could have the suite."

"Seems so, doesn't it?" Then they laughed together.

"Would you allow me to buy you a drink, Hatsuko-san?"

"I am not supposed to, but who will know?" she answered. At the ten o'clock hour, she went and turned off the lounge lights and locked the cash drawers. Then she turn toward Latoure and said, "Are you ready to go?"

"Yes, of course, I have some rum in my room if you are interested?" She thought it over in her mind as they walked to the elevator after locking the doors to the lounge. Once on the elevator, she pressed floor eleven only. *I guess that answers my question,* he thought to himself.

She continued her duties as bartender, mixing the drinks and telling Latoure where the ice machine was and what door it was behind on this floor. He had no problem completing his ice bucket detail. Upon returning to his room, Hatsuko had changed into one of the kimono-type robes and sat, waiting on the ice so she could finish mixing the rum and cokes.

"Don't look so surprised, Larry." Her English was as perfect as anyone in the States. "Your reputation has been talked about ever since your first night." Now it was his turn to be surprised at the events of the evening. Should he continue down this path or respect what relationship he and Johnny had established. She brought him out of his deep thought by saying, "Drink your drink, then we take a shower, my friend." She was truly a beautiful woman, so he lifted his glass to hers, clinking it; they drank them straight down.

They took an intimate shower together, followed by a couple of hours of exploring one another's bodies. Hatsuko was filled with pent-up passion and took every advantage of Latoure's sexual prowess. Not sure how long it was or even caring how long, he brought her to his chest after their lovemaking. She laid her head upon it as they both fell into a deep sleep. Sometime during that night or early morning, Hatsuko awoke and slipped from his suite, returning to her room. It was around 9:00 a.m. when he finally got up and joined the rest of the masses. He called for room service and his pot of coffee. Hatsuko took his call and told him it was about time he got up and thanked him for a wonderful evening. He told her he felt the same. It would be a night he would always remember fondly.

After drinking his fill of coffee, he began packing up all his gear. Both he and Scully would be leaving the following morning from Yakota Air Base. He checked his remaining money, which was all in US Dollars. There was still almost $1,000 left; more than enough for his evening with Jamie. He busied himself straightening out the suite, even though he knew housekeeping would clean up after him. He went downstairs to the Front Desk, asking where he could exchange $200 for yen. The clerk told him that he would be happy to accommodate him. Now the only thing left was to wait until 5:00 p.m. for Jamie's arrival.

He went for a walk outside the Hotel; he had been in Tokyo for almost a week and didn't know what was around the block. A local grocery store, a small Mom-and-Pop noodle shop, and many apartment-type buildings were to be found in the direction he took; then he did an about-face and walked back past the hotel to see what was available in the other direction. It looked to be about the same. There was another restaurant; this one had wax images of what they specialized in like he had seen on Okinawa. Office building, furniture, and a few more apartments. He decided to try the restaurant and the tonkatsu. He remembered that it was a pork cutlet with vegetables over a bowl of rice. He told the woman in the best Japanese he could, "Tonkatsu, dozo." This proved to be a mistake because she began speaking Japanese to him, believing he understood. He just shook his head and kept repeating, "Hai, Hai, Hai!" The lunch came to 500 yen or about $2 US; he paid with yen.

Johnny was at the front desk when he returned to the Hotel. He stopped by to say hello and let him know he had a guest stopping by later in the day. "A 'round eye' girl I met on Tuesday, Johnny. A real looker." Apparently, Johnny knew nothing about where his daughter spent last night, and for that, Latoure was thankful. "We are checking out in the morning, Johnny, and catching a flight back to Vietnam at noon. What do we owe you? Let me settle up with you now."

Johnny seemed surprised at the question but replied, "You, my friend, owe me nothing. That Johnnie Walker Black would have paid for a month's stay here. Your friend rang up a lot of room service. It seems he and Yumiko spent most of their time in the room."

"I will tell him to come see you soon." Then Latoure offered his hand in friendship.

He swung by Scully's room, who answered, wrapped in a towel. "Hey, Army Guy, go settle up with Johnny so we can just leave in the morning to catch our flight."

"Sure, will do. Let me throw something on, and I will do it now," Scully answered.

"Thanks, man." And Latoure walked down the hall to his room. He spent some time primping his face and clothes, wanting to impress Jamie when she arrived. It was four thirty; not much longer. He turned on the radio and began listening to some music on Armed Forces Radio. His phone rang about five minutes past five. Johnny told him his guest was on her way up and thanked Latoure for sending Scully down to pay his bill.

"I hope to see you on my way out, Johnny. If not, thank you for an outstanding R&R."

As he hung up, there was a soft knock on his door. Jamie stood in the doorway with a smile on her face, wearing a trench coat that she was holding open. She was totally nude except for a small shoulder bag by her side.

"Cat got your tongue, Marine?" she said, laughing. He stepped aside, and she almost floated by him.

Not more than three or four steps inside, he grabbed her wrist and turned her toward him. His hands went around her waist and placed his lips upon hers. An hour later, they both lay nude on the bed, cuddling.

"Are you ready for a night on the town or should we just order room service?" Jamie asked him.

"I want to treat you to a night on the town wherever you want to go. As long as I am back to catch my flight in the morning at Yakota."

"Oh, I didn't know you were at the end of your R&R, but we will make the most of it, but first—" Jamie was insatiable. He knew not the reason why but was pleased at the results. Another hour passed before they went and gave one another a sponge bath and rinse. She had come prepared with a beautiful cocktail dress, thigh highs, and heels. He was glad he still had the sports coat they let him borrow; dressed to kill, off they went to their night in *Tokyo After Dark*.

It looked like his R&R had come full circle as Jamie told the taxi driver in perfect Japanese to take them to Roppongi. Their final destination would be the Blue Note Jazz Club, often referred to as the "Little Brother" to the Original in London, England. It was a high-end establishment; however, it did offer world-renowned acts. This particular evening's artist was someone known to Latoure and most likely to Jamie as well. Playboy's Number One Baritone Saxophone Artist, Gerry Mulligan. Latoure told Jamie he played the baritone sax during his high school junior and senior years, which made it extra special to hear Mulligan play live. They also grazed on appetizers, which were more akin to entrées, as they enjoyed the entertainment.

During a set break, Jamie excused herself and told Latoure she needed a bathroom break. None the wiser, he held down the table. Around five minutes later, she returned but not alone; she had Mr.

Mulligan in tow and introduced him to Latoure. He told him that rumor had it that Latoure was also a baritone sax player as well.

"That was five years ago, Mr. Mulligan," Latoure said.

"Gerry, please. I understand that you are headed back to Vietnam in the morning?"

"That's right, sir." He was still in awe to be talking with his musical idol face-to-face.

"Well then, that settles it. You are going to join the quartet for at least one song," Gerry replied.

Jamie sat next to Latoure with a huge smile on her face. She had met Mulligan the day before at the Playboy Club and was his waitress that evening.

"One song only, Gerry, and it has to be 'Three Blind Mice.' It is the only song I remember playing off your album with my fellow jazz players," Latoure told Mr. Mulligan.

"Can do. Easy," Gerry said, sliding out from the table and heading back to the stage.

"Ladies and Gentlemen, I have a treat for Us this evening. A Marine friend is here on R&R from Vietnam. He also is a baritone sax player, and I shamed him into joining the quartet for one song. Sergeant Latoure, if you please."

Latoure wasn't sure how this was going to go, but never one to turn down a challenge, up to the stage he went; the eyes of the paying customers were following his every step. Gerry handed him the sax and strap to put around his neck then picked up the clarinet. The only recognizable part of the song "Three Blind Mice" was the first eight bars or so; the rest was off in a jazz world, playing whatever came to mind. On Gerry's count, off they went. Latoure was happy that he hadn't lost his aperture, so the mouthpiece rested easily on his lower lip. The sax was top-of-the-line, as one would expect, so the five or six minutes of "Three Blind Mice" went off without any errors.

He handed the sax back to Mr. Mulligan and thanked him for the opportunity to play with him. In return, Gerry told Latoure that he was happy to let a fellow sax player and that it was an awesome experience. The crowd was applauding like crazy as Latoure made his way back to Jamie. Then the dam broke; drinks were being sent to their table by just about everyone in the club. It was more than they could drink in a week, much less the rest of the evening. Jamie leaned in, kissed him on the cheek, patted his thigh, then lifted a glass, and clinked it with his before drinking.

The remainder of the evening was a blur. Customers stopped by their table, shook hands, or patted his back; but Latoure felt it was mostly to get a closer look at Jamie. She looked stunning. He was more interested in her companionship and listening to Gerry Mulligan. Around 2:00 a.m., she said they should be leaving before the crowd left the club. So arm in arm, he escorted his beautiful date out of the lounge. He wasn't concerned about getting any sleep, knowing the plane ride back to Vietnam would offer him some time. He knew he needed to drink some water; his father had told him drink plenty of water after a night's drinking or even better, add water in the drink. He was drinking whiskey water at the Blue Note but told Jamie he needed coffee or water now.

She hailed a taxi, and soon they were at the Perfect Room. She told the front desk clerk that Latoure needed tons of coffee. The clerk acknowledged with a "Hai so desu."

It was Hatsuko, but Latoure was too far gone to focus on who Jamie was talking to. Once inside the suite, Jamie stripped him and began a regiment of cold-water sprays from the handheld showerhead. He was not really sure how much time passed, but he began to realize he was back at his suite naked and being drenched with cold water.

Now with the ability to speak coherently, he told Jamie perhaps ten times in a row, "Thank you for a very special evening."

The coffee had been delivered while Jamie was trying to sober Latoure up; so wrapped in a towel, he sat drinking cup after cup. His world was slowly coming into focus; the coffee was helping.

"What time is it?" he asked her.

"Almost six," she answered.

"I am sorry. I never intended on drinking that much," he told her.

"I knew that, but heck, it was free, right?" she said, laughing. "I am going to leave now, Larry. I wrote my address here in Tokyo plus my address at the university. You can write me at either address. Please do so. I need to know you are all right."

He was now sober enough to notice the tears forming in her eyes. He leaned next to her and kissed the tear that began to run down her cheek. She arose and was gone in an instant.

He called the front desk to order something to eat. Hatsuko answered, took his breakfast order, and asked if he was okay. He told her he was fine now but had too much to drink at the Blue Note last night. Now she understood why a "round eye" brought him back in the early morning. Many foreigners went to the Blue Note.

About seven thirty, his breakfast was delivered by Hatsuko, telling him her father had taken over the front desk. Johnny thought that after delivering Latoure's breakfast, Hatsuko would just go to her own room, but that was the furthest thing from her mind at the time. She sat and drank coffee while Latoure filled his stomach with the last real meal he would be eating for the next six months. He suddenly realized he was wrapped only in a towel and stood up to go change. Hatsuko had other ideas as she grabbed the towel and pulled it from his waist then moved in his arms, kissing him longingly and deeply.

Hatsuko was pleased that he reacted positively to her touch and kisses. Leading him by the hand toward the bed, which had been thankfully made by housekeeping after they left for the club. The next hour, he gave his very being to her, loving every inch of her body again and again. As she lay upon his chest, he looked at the clock. It was a little past nine; time to dress and finish packing.

"Hatsuko-chan, I have to get ready to leave now. We don't have that much time to get to Yakota." She lay there totally nude, tempting him to join her, but time was limited. Finally, all dressed and his bag packed to the gills, he said, "It's time, Hatsuko-chan."

She got up from the bed still nude and hugged him tightly. With a final kiss goodbye, he turned to leave, and she finally spoke, "Sayonara, Larry."

He looked back over his shoulder at her nude form and made a mental note of her beauty.

Scully was walking down the hallway with Yumiko alongside. "Sarge, I had a super time. I need to thank you a lot."

"No problem, Army Guy," he answered.

They swung by the front desk to shake Johnny's hand and give him heartfelt thanks from both; Johnny had called a taxi for them, and it was waiting out front.

Yakota Air Force Base was about a twenty-minute ride; both had to present their military IDs at the front gate before being waved through. The taxi driver had driven military to the terminal before, so without any further delay, he pulled up to the main doors. They asked how much, and the taxi driver told them, "My brother has paid."

"Johnny is your brother?" Latoure asked and got a nod from the driver.

"Safe trip, GIs!"

At the Check-In Counter, they were told what gate and at what time the Military Flight would be leaving. Latoure asked what sort of a Military Flight; to which the clerk answered, KC-130. It was the standard turboprop of the Vietnam era; however, there would be no stewardess nor soft seats for their return trip. They both picked up some candy bars and chips at the snack bar and sought out their gate. Promptly at noon, the aircraft began to load, once again, by rank. To Latoure's mind, a C-130 made no difference; all sat in web seats along the outer side of the plane.

There was cargo aboard, all netted and strapped down; their seats were directly next to it. The netting would make a nice footrest when they leaned back. Their personal bags were between them, which also provided a place to rest. The engines roared as the aircraft taxied to the end of the runway. The power pushed them against their bags when the pilot pointed the plane almost straight up. The hum of the engines put both to sleep almost immediately. Latoure felt a hand shake him; it was Scully telling them it was time to strap in for landing. They soon found out why. The aircraft made a combat landing into Da Nang twenty thousand feet to the deck, and they were back in-Country.

CHAPTER 7
Moving Day: Hills 55 and 37

Latoure was lucky once again. There was a truck sent by the First Battalion to pick up a couple of Marines returning from R&R, so with little difficulty, he managed to get a ride back with them. One of the Marines remembered him from the Mother's Day attack, so it was almost like old home week, discussing that day's events plus the pleasures found on R&R. The conversation helped him to get his mind partially straight and back into the war. Additionally, the smells and the looks of the locals as they stared at the Marines while the truck slowly rolled through the Dog Patch was motivation enough to get his mind right. The farther down Highway 1 they rolled, the more his senses picked up.

He dropped his bag off at the S-2 before walking across the compound to the S-1 so he could turn in his R&R orders. Staff Sergeant Stone asked him how it went. Latoure told the Admin Chief that he would let him know when they played bridge again. Stone told him that was going to be awhile, so Latoure inquired, "Why? What's up?"

"Check with your boss. He has all the info," Stone answered.

"Thanks, Staff Sergeant Stone. I will catch up with you sometime and give you all the hot details." He was wondering what in the heck was going on for the Admin Chief to be so cryptic.

Still in his Dress Uniform, he returned to the S-2. The Captain was waiting for his return from the S-1.

"Sit down, Sergeant." The Captain told him then continued, "Go put your Jungles on and don't bother unpacking. The Regiment is moving out tonight to Hill 55. It is part of the drawdown. The

Third Division is pulling out of country, and the First Division is going to cover the entire I Corps. We have intel that the enemy knows and plans on attacking here tonight after we pull out at dusk. We will move a Company of Marines and ROK Marines to cover the perimeter to surprise them as part of the move."

"Holly shit, Skipper. Seems like I just got back in time," Latoure told the Intelligence Officer.

Who then said, "We were waiting for your return we couldn't do it without the Regimental Sharpshooter! Not really, but that sounded good." The Captain said, laughing. "The Gunny and Ski are at Hill 55 now, cleaning up the new S-2 and the Scout Hooch. Get changed and return with your gear we will pack out from here."

When he got to the Scouts' Hut, it was empty on their side, and on his side, all his gear was stacked in a neat pile by the door. He changed quickly then went to the armory and picked up all three of his weapons: M16, shotgun, and .45 pistol. He returned to the Hooch and grabbed his B-4 after stuffing his R&R goodies inside. He must have looked like a hobo walking back to the Intelligence Hut with weapons and bags hanging off his body. Private First Class Hitt had all the field desk packed up and the maps covered with brown paper. Latoure helped Hitt stack the desks by the front entrance next to his personal gear. Now they waited until dusk.

The Gunny and Ski returned in the S-2 jeep, followed by a six-by-six truck with the Scouts in the rear. Less than twenty minutes later, the truck was packed. At dusk the convoy of six-by-sixes began filing out of the old regimental headquarters; while at the same time, different six-by-sixes dropped off the surprise for the enemy. Mike Company had the honor, and some very mean-looking ROK Marines were waiting for the attack as they snuck into the perimeter bunkers.

Latoure had no idea which way they were going to reach Hill 55; there was the safe way and the not-so-safe way through the edge of Dodge City. They tried to stay hidden behind all the desk and equipment so the enemy would be none the wiser. The trip to Hill 55 was uneventful, and just as quickly, the truck was unloaded and staged to be unpacked in the morning. The Scouts helped him carry his gear to the new intel Scout Hooch. As they got closer, Latoure noticed a huge berm on the back side of the hut and thought it would keep the small arms from popping through the screen like the old hut. He stopped just before entering and said out loud, "Shit, we have lost our shower, haven't we?"

Kirby answered, "Yeah, that really sucks. The Mama-san seems cool though."

For the remainder of the evening, he staged his gear. This Hooch had a shelf running along the inside at about eye level, and Latoure thought it was a good place for his shaving kit and helmet, so he didn't have to dig them out when he needed them. Just before 22:00, he stretched out on his rack. The new Mama-san had blown up his air mattress, for which he was thankful. As sleep came over him, visions of Tokyo floated through his mind. Promptly at 22:00, an explosion went off just outside the Hooch; the concussion caused his helmet to fly off the small ledge and land directly on his chest. Latoure thought that was it, and there was a huge hole in his chest, forgetting where he had placed his helmet.

It took him longer than normal to come to his senses; more than likely just a few seconds longer, realizing that it was his helmet, not a hole in his chest. The Scouts were at the ready as well, expecting an enemy attack at any time. They all moved to the edge of the berm, looking toward the outside perimeter. What came into view was a huge 175 mm artillery piece firing rounds toward Charlie Ridge. This type of fire was Interdicting Fire, which dropped rounds on known enemy trails and rally points. They looked at one another, shaking their heads collectively, and returned to the hut. M16 rounds provided makeshift earplugs for the remainder of the night.

At first light, Private First Class Hitt came running down the hill, yelling for Sergeant Latoure. "The Skipper needs you ASAP," (as soon as possible) he told Latoure.

"What's going on, Hitt?"

"I don't know, Sarge. He was really pissed and shocked the hell out of me when he told me to come get you," Hitt answered.

Latoure didn't even shave as both Marines double-timed back up the slope to the S-2.

"Two things," the Captain began. "First, the enemy was completely surprised that we were waiting for them at the old compound. The second, the six-by-six carrying the Third Battalion's Intelligence was blown up on the way to Hill 37, their new compound."

"Anybody hurt?" Latoure asked the Intelligence Officer.

"The six-by-six Driver was killed outright, but the Intel people were riding on top of their gear, so concussions and shrapnel got all of them. They will be hospitalized for a while; the Intel Chief got the worst of it, so you are now it."

"What are you saying, Skipper?" Latoure asked.

"You are going to the Third Battalion on TAD [temporary additional duty], which makes it official until the Gunny is released from the Hospital. Go grab your gear. Ski will drive you to Hill 37."

"Aye, aye, Skipper. Can I take Kirby and Can with me?" Latoure was glad the Skipper approved his request, at least there would be two friendly faces with him. As he ran down the hill to get his gear, he yelled at Kirby and Can to grab their gear; they were coming with him. Ski had already told them what happened to the Third Battalion Intelligence Section, so both were ready to leave.

The Captain told both Latoure and Ski to use Highway 1 Delta because Latoure was needed immediately. He told Ski, "Do not return the same way alone. Hook up with a convoy coming back this way or take the long way back, which was exactly the way the Third Battalion intel was driving when they got blown up. Keep your eyes peeled and be ready for anything." Finally, he told Latoure, "I know you men will do us proud."

Off they went, heading for Hill 37. During the drive, Ski told them the scuttlebutt was that it was a 250-pound bomb buried in the road on a command-detonated fuse which got the Third Battalion. Ski didn't waste any time leaving Hill 37; he knew to travel the highways of Vietnam at night was a ticket to hell.

The two Intel Scouts took off in search of their assigned Hooch and told Latoure they would return to see what was happening after they stowed all their personal gear. Upon entering the Bunker/Fort atop Hill 37, an eerie feeling came over him. The French were the last to man this hilltop fortification. During the French collapse at Dien Bien Phu in 1954, the French Detachment at Hill 37 was overran, and many of them perished. Perhaps the ghosts of those fallen French soldiers still walked the corridors.

The intelligence section of the Seventh Marines had placed what remained of the Third Battalion's S-2 equipment and desks that weren't completely destroyed when the truck was blown up inside. Latoure spent the next two hours with Kirby's and Can's help trying to put the S-2 in some form of order plus hooking up the communications gear for the intelligence net. There was no one to represent the Third Battalion S-2 that wasn't in the Hospital; they were it.

It was well past 22:00 when the S-2 was finally squared away. Latoure told the Scouts he would see them right after he did the radio check on the Intel net. Before the Scouts got to leave, a huge figure of a Marine stood in the doorway, blocking their exit.

"Which one of you is Latoure?" Both Scouts pointed at Latoure without saying a word; their eyes were bulging from their heads.

"Sergeant Major Gimplemen. The Colonel wants to see you in the tower, Sergeant."

Latoure told the Sergeant Major, "We are done here."

"Outstanding" was the reply, followed by "This way, Sergeant."

Latoure climbed the ladder up into the top of the Old French Fort and through a trap door which opened to a sandbagged lookout. The figure was peering through a Starlight scope at something in the Village below. An M14 with Starlight lay on top of the sandbag wall.

"Sergeant Latoure reporting as ordered, sir."

"So you are the deadly marksman that Colonel Vreeland told me about," Lieutenant Colonel White said.

"Excuse me, sir?" Latoure replied.

"Colonel Vreeland told me all about Mother's Day and what you did that night."

"Just doing my duty, sir."

"I want you to shoot that VC down in Dia Loc taking a crap." The Colonel pointed in the general direction of the suspected VC.

Latoure didn't want to shoot anyone, especially before he had a chance to visit the Village; hell, that might be the Village chief. "Sir, I am not familiar with this M14, where it is zeroed, to three hundred or five hundred meters. Also at this time, I do not know the distance from here to the Village."

"Did you hear my order, Sergeant? It wasn't a request. It was an order." Given no way out, Latoure picked up the M14, sighting in on the squatting figure an unknown distance away. He fired one round, and immediately, the phone rang. He picked it up, and the Eleventh Marines 105 mm gun emplacement was on the other end telling him that his shot was short, impacting just outside their position. Latoure apologized then sighted in on the VC again. The Village roofs were made of tin, so he thought if he hit the roof, the VC would run away. This shot was on target, rattling the tin roof, and off ran the target.

"Sorry, Sir, I just wasn't familiar with this M14. May I leave now, sir?"

The Colonel looked at Latoure with fire in his eyes and said, "Get out of here." Which Latoure gladly complied with.

The Third Battalion had just arrived on Hill 37, so he felt that the Colonel could not have known who that person was or anything about the surrounding area. Latoure knew he needed to visit Dia Loc and the surrounding area to see what side the people were on. He passed by the Sergeant Major, shaking his head, and the Sergeant Major gave him a slap on the back, which almost knocked the wind out of him. Latoure felt that perhaps his duties as the Intel Chief here at the Third Battalion wasn't going to be what he had hoped.

Kirby or Can had scrounged up midrats from somewhere; there was a brown paper bag with baloney sandwiches and orange and some kind of Kool-Aid drink inside. He was glad that they were looking out for him, and he would do the same for them. He kicked off his jungle boots and lay on top of the cot; no Mama-san to blow up his air mattress, if they even remembered to bring them. Before he realized it, the sun was rising and shining directly on his face. Lesson learned. Tonight, his head would be on the other end of the cot; hopefully this time, with an air mattress.

L. R. LAVANCHER

As he was completing his morning hygiene, Kirby came up to him, escorting two Marines and a Kit Carson Scout named Quan. Fortunately for them, they were a part of the advance party and were not riding on the truck when it was blown up. He shook their hands and told them to standby and that more than likely, they would be going into Dia Loc this morning. As they were turning to leave, Can came walking up; immediately, the two Kit Carson Scouts locked eyes, and if looks could kill, one of them would be dead. As soon as the group was out of earshot, Latoure asked Can what the problem with the Kit Carson Scout was. Can only replied, "He number 10. No good!"

Can was a former North Vietnamese Warrant Officer, as was Tang; special dispensation was given to both of them so they could become Kit Carson Scouts. Latoure trusted Can and even Tang, for that matter, with his life, which had been proven during Pipestone Canyon by Can. He didn't want to be prejudged, but if Can didn't like him, there was a good reason. It was something he definitely would look into.

There was no Intelligence Officer assigned to the battalion by the operations officer. Major Thurston's secondary MOS was 0202, while his primary was 0301 Infantry Officer. At least the two of them spoke some of the same language. Latoure told him what happened with the Colonel last evening, but the Major didn't comment; he just took in the information. Latoure asked the Major who would he need to get permission from to go into Dia Loc for a liaison visit. The answer was simple; it was the Major, who quickly gave Latoure permission to take his Scouts to Dia Loc. Additionally, he asked the Major about Quan the Kit Carson Scout. The Major told him that he had just recently joined prior to the move to Hill 37 and volunteered for the advance party. Piece by piece, Latoure was beginning to analyze the bits of information in an opinion; the question was, Was it because of Can's dislike for the scout named Quan?

Corporal Kirby approached with two Intel Scouts and the two Kit Carsons. Latoure told Kirby to give him five minutes, and they would be on their way to Dia Loc, and to do an equipment check if he hadn't done it yet. Kirby looked at Latoure with a quizzical look, knowing that Latoure normally did that, but told Latoure it was no problem. Latoure went back inside to the S-2 and called the Regiment. Gunny Sparks answered, and Latoure requested that the Gunny find out as much information about Quan as possible. Of course, the Gunny wanted to know what was up; Latoure answered that he was working on something that didn't seem quite right with Quan. He also told the Gunny they were going to do a face-to-face in Dia Loc and that Latoure would check back when they returned.

"We're all set, Sergeant Latoure. This is Lance Corporal Knight and Private First Class Wright."

Latoure shook their hands and then said, "Saddle up!"

It was less than one thousand meters outside the perimeter where the Village of Dia Loc outskirts began. The villager's eyes bore a hole into the group as they passed through with smiles on their faces. Latoure headed toward the hut where the VC was seen the night before. As he suspected, the hut belonged to the Base Barber and not a VC. He was glad that his aim was off. He asked Can to find out where the Village Chief lived and led the group to it.

As they approached, the Village Chief's head was bobbing like a bobblehead doll, shaking up and down with a huge smile on his face until his eye caught Quan. Just like turning off a lamp, the Chief's mannerism changed from friendly to standoffish.

Latoure's senses kicked into overdrive and said, "That's it. We are going back in."

Kirby asked, "What's up, Sarge?"

"Later" was the answer.

The total trip to and back from Dia Loc took less than an hour. When the team reached the compound, Latoure told them to take the rest of the day off then turned to Kirby and Can. "You two, with me."

A second after they stepped into the Battalion S-2, Latoure looked at Can. "What do you know about Quan?"

"He not same Quan I know from KCS School. I no like him. He problem."

"Kirby, have you heard Quan say anything or do something off-color since we got here?"

Kirby answered, "Not really but I haven't been around him that much."

Latoure then asked, "Did you see the look on the Village Chief when he saw Quan?"

"Sorry, Sarge, I was looking around for threats. I didn't notice anything."

Can quickly said, "I see. I know he was scared."

"Okay, you two keep an eye on him but not so he sees you watching." They acknowledged Latoure with a nod and headed down to the Scouts' Hooch.

Latoure went in to talk to the Major and drop a bomb on him. "Sir, I believe Quan is a VC spy."

The Major replied with a look of amazement, "What did you just say, Sergeant Latoure?"

"I believe Quan is a VC plant." Latoure explained his reasons and that he had Gunny Sparks were checking on a couple things as well.

"Stand at ease, Sergeant. In fact, grab a squat." The Major rang up the Division and asked to be put through to KCS School. As he waited, he told Latoure that one of the Instructors was a friend from Basic School. Latoure listened as the two caught up on old times before Major Thurston asked about Quan. The Major repeated aloud as his fellow classmate talked about Quan. "He was from Dia Loc, Chu Hoi'd when the Q-Eighty-Second was surrounded by Seventh Marines in Elephant Valley last year. Late twenties, not married, excellent student."

Latoure interrupted, "Did you say late twenties?" The Major nodded. "Our Quan is late thirties. Two-inch scar on his face right side."

"No scar you said?" Asking his friend to say again. "No scar," the Major repeated. "Thanks, buddy, I have a problem to take care of. Talk to you again."

"Damn, Latoure, you are good. Less than forty-eight hours, you find a VC spy." The Major then told him, "Get all the Scouts up here at 1300. Tell them I need to brief them about an Operation we are planning."

"Aye, aye, sir." As Latoure left, the Major picked up the phone and called the Division Provost Marshal. Latoure went to the Scouts' Hooch and told them about the meeting with the Major at 1300 and then said, "Let's go get some chow together. We can tell stories as we eat." He was trying his best to act like nothing was out of the ordinary.

Waiting inside the conference room were two Criminal Investigators, two huge Military Polices, and the Major; all of them were armed with .45 pistols, waiting for the Scouts. The Major had told everyone of the men to get out of the bunker and stay gone until at least 1430. As soon as the Scouts entered the conference room, the two MPs grabbed Quan, immobilizing him. The CID had brought a fingerprint kit and proceeded to fingerprint Quan, whose face by this time was very pale and sweating like crazy.

"Sergeant Latoure," the Major said, "give your Scouts the day off, but you stay!" No other words were spoken, none were needed, as the Intel Scouts left the room.

Fingerprints were matched against the initial set taken from the real Quan when he surrendered. The CID, with a loop, matched the two sets, and as suspected, they did not match. Quan was then handcuffed and removed by the two MPs, followed closely by the CID after shaking hands with first the Major then Latoure. Latoure thought to himself that he would never be privy to the final outcome of the arrest but was glad it was over. After the law enforcement types left, Latoure briefed the Major in greater detail how he came to suspect Quan, beginning with Can's dislike and the Village chief's expressions. He asked permission to return to Dia Loc the following morning and was quickly given permission by the Major.

The next three weeks were sort of a letdown after the incident with Quan; it was filled with intelligence Summaries to the Regiment until the day before the Gunny was to be released from the Hospital. Can had been talking to the locals who worked in and around Hill 37 and was told about a cache of weapons north of the base, somewhere on the banks of the river. Once again, the Major gave approval to the Intel Scouts and Latoure to check out the information. As they were checking along the banks of the Dia Loc River for the reported cache, a call for help came over the radio.

Across the river, two snipers had gotten themselves into a fix and were surrounded by VCs. Latoure could hear the firefight and thought they were just about 1,500 meters from the action. Can, in the meantime, had grabbed a Mama-san and her sampan to take the five-man team to the northern bank. Latoure called in on the radio the Scouts' intention when, almost immediately, a reply came back, "Gunsmoke 2, this is Gunsmoke actual. You are to hold your position. Mike Company is en route."

Latoure knew where Mike Company was operating, and he also knew that it would be at least an hour before they reached the Snipers. "Gunsmoke, this is Gunsmoke 2, copy your last."

All the Scouts looked at Latoure in disbelief. He had no answer to their obvious questions.

Later that evening, Latoure was on the radio sending out the daily Intelligence Summary when a Marine walked into the S-2 and laid a bloody Model 40 sniper rifle on the desk. The Marine then said, "We weren't in time. The Sniper and his spotter were killed."

Latoure's blood began to boil as he picked up the weapon and headed down the passageway to the Commanding Officer. The saloon-type doors made a crashing sound as he burst into the CO's office. Not too softly, he slammed the weapon on the desk and began to blame the CO for the snipers' deaths. The Colonel was about to throw Latoure into the brig for disrespect when two huge hands clamped down on Latoure's arms, lifting him off his feet and physically carrying him out of the office; using Latoure as a battering ram, once again slamming the saloon doors open.

"Cool down, Sergeant Latoure. You may have been right, but now was not the time to confront the CO," the Battalion Sergeant Major said. Latoure was still shaking with rage over the needless deaths of the two Marines. Then the Sergeant Major reached in his desk and took out some scotch, pouring two separate glasses. "Let's drink to them, Sergeant Latoure."

Lifting his glass, Latoure tapped his with the Sergeant Major's and said, "Go with God, Marines. Semper Fi." They drank the scotch in one gulp.

Nothing further came from that incident, and Latoure was happy to see the Intel Chief returning to his duties from the hospital. Latoure briefed the Gunny on what transpired during his watch. They shook hands as Latoure sat in the jeep that brought the Gunny, who told the driver to take Latoure and his two Scouts back to Hill 55. The ride was made in silence; all three were still upset at the deaths of the two Marines. Latoure had mixed feelings about returning to Hill 55, having had a taste as a Battalion Intelligence Chief. Who knew what lay in the days ahead?

CHAPTER 8
Return to Hill 55:
The Mid-Watch

Latoure would have liked his return to Hill 55 to have a little more to it. Such as it was with the First Marine Division, he was being tasked with the entire I Corps area after the withdrawal of the Third Marine Division. Unit assignments were made by replacing the Division Area Of Responsibilities with that of a Regiment and Battalions replacing AORs of Regiments; one could say the Marine Units were stretched very thin. The Intelligence Officer told Latoure he would be manning the watch from Midnight to 0800 with his main responsibility of receiving incoming raw intelligence, Intelligence Summaries (INTSUMS) and finally controlling access to the Command Operations Center (COC).

The COC was a huge bunker buried beneath stacks of sandbags and logs very close to the Military Crest, which placed it about fifty meters from the crest. You entered down a set of very steep stairs, which made one feel like you were entering a cave. At the bottom right was the intelligence desk, to the left was the Commanding Officer's, and directly behind the intel desk sat the operations officer. The length was about twenty-four feet with a width of twelve feet. There was a secondary entrance or exit on the far end of the bunker. This area was covered by the Korean Marine Liaison and Marine Corps Artillery. Maps of the area outside Hill 55 filled every square inch of the bulkheads.

Latoure sat at a military field desk with a shelving directly to his front, filled with blank forms and the Covered Intelligence

Net. This net was the same radio and cipher unit he carried during Operation Pipestone Canyon, so its operation was not unfamiliar to him. For safety purposes, no weapons were allowed in the confined space of the bunker, except a couple of .45s on a few officer's hips. Latoure's Ka-Bar knife stuck into the four-by-four wooden beam that arched the lower entrance was his protection. *Better than nothing,* he thought. Within the first two or three hours, most of the intelligence traffic was received, compiled, and then forwarded to the Division G-2.

The Intel Scouts were kept busy supporting other Regimental Units who were patrolling around Hill 55. Latoure really missed not going into the bush, as it was called. The Regimental Operations Officer's name was Ramsey. A Career Ground Pounder with a penance for military history and chess. During Latoure's High School, he was a member of the Chess Club, but Major Ramsey was way above Latoure's level. Upon the corner of the Major's desk sat a stack of Chess Books. Latoure asked if he could borrow one of them to read.

"Oh, so you play, Latoure?" the Major asked.

"A very long time ago, sir," Latoure answered. Of course, the Major, not knowing Latoure's reputation within the Intelligence Business, had no idea what Latoure had planned.

Mid-Rations were delivered to those manning the different desks within the COC. Five-gallon jugs filled with Ice Tea or Kool-Aid, which was referred to as "Bug Juice" by Marines, was the main offering for drinks. Latoure was a coffee drinker; coffee was given to him by a Scout that wasn't assigned to a unit. The food was baloney and cheese sandwiches with mustard, and on a rare occasion, peanut butter and jelly with potato chips. Even though there was no daily contact with his Scouts, communications were passed with those remaining behind. He felt like he should do something special for them as soon as he could.

Latoure's research within the Major's Chess Books proved to be fruitful. He memorized two different obscure checkmate moves by two of the masters from long ago, planning to surprise Major Ramsey with them. He chose the one that took him longer to memorize to try first. He had to come to the COC early to play the Major before his watch began, having set up the match the night before. Wouldn't you know, that was the evening the VC decided to send a couple Lob Bombs to welcome the First Marines to the area. A very load thud was heard at the entrance; immediately, the Regimental Commander ordered, "EVERYONE OUT!"

Rapidly, all left through the secondary entrance or exit. Luckily, the 250-pound bomb did not detonate; in fact, of the three Lob Bombs, only one did explode. Unfortunately, a Marine who was asleep and was leaving the very next morning back to the world was not as lucky. A piece of shrapnel the size of a dime had gone through the side of his hut then through his air mattress and sliced his jugular. Nothing could be done for him. EOD (Explosive Ordnance Detail) had the bomb de-armed and quickly removed. Latoure checked on his Scouts while EOD did their job; all were okay.

Latoure apologized to the Major for their interrupted game and set up a return match the following evening at 2200. Latoure felt he had made enough moves to reveal what his intentions were, so he reread the second attack again. A negative on Hill 55 was the new Regimental Executive Officer, who was responsible for the security of Hill 55. The XO set Condition 2, which meant all would sleep in the bunkers with 50 percent remaining awake while the others slept in the bunkers. That decision was way above Latoure's pay grade. The next evening, he did win the chess match against Major Ramsey, much to his surprise, using the Queen's sacrifice. A move quite common now but obscure in the late '60s.

Days turned into weeks, and Hill 55 was still on Condition 2. Not to be one to sit on his hands, Latoure began to research why the XO made that decision. It didn't take long to find out that First Radio Battalion had intercepted traffic saying the T-Sixty-Ninth Sapper Battalion was going to attack in force. Latoure didn't blame the XO for not knowing the 1-Sixty-Ninth was no longer an effective unit because it was decimated to the man on Mother's Day. For whatever the reason, the XO refused to listen, plus the Regimental Commander had just found out he was to be promoted to Brigadier General and wouldn't interfere. Hill 55 was abuzz with rumors concerning the XO; Latoure tried his best to control the Marines' anger. Colonel

Wilkerson was to take command of the Regiment soon, and Latoure tried to get the troops to wait until then. It wasn't to be the case. There was an Officer's or SNCO's single-seat toilet close to the COC. Like clockwork the XO took his dump at or about 2230 every night. Someone had floated gasoline on top of the normal diesel, knowing the XO smoked a cigar during his nightly visit. It didn't explode but sent up a hell of a flame. The XO wasn't really hurt; he received a closer shave below the waist. Shortly thereafter, Condition 3 was set.

Latoure felt he needed to do something special for the Scouts, so instead of hitting the rack, he drove the Intel jeep to Freedom Hill Exchange, specifically the Package Store. He was too young to pass for a Staff Noncommissioned Officer but could instead pass for a second Lieutenant. A ration Card was created for Second Lieutenant Smyth, H. E. to use at the Package Store. He picked up three cases of Black Label Beer, the only US Beer available in-country, plus two bottles of Jack Daniel's. Paid with the script, he headed out the door. Then Murphy's Law hit him square in the face. Both the Regimental Operations Officer, Major Ramsey, and the Regimental Sergeant Major, who Latoure had never met as of yet, were entering the Package Store.

With strength he did not know he had, Latoure lifted the cases from his waist, bottles balancing on top, so his hands covered the second Lieutenant's Bars he was wearing. Visions of Court-Martial passed through his mind. Luckily, nothing was said. Latoure lowered the booze into the jeep and made a hasty retreat back to Hill 55.

That evening while playing chess, the Major said, "Don't let it happen again!"

With a sigh of relief and nothing further being said, they continued to play chess almost nightly. Latoure was the only person who could beat the Major even if it was only one out of ten matches; whether that had any bearing, he did not know or did not ask.

Latoure sometimes got a reprieve from his Midnight watch duties especially if it was a Civil Action Operation, which involved almost all the Scouts, not just one or two. This operations involved a Company-sized unit or larger if necessary. Under the cover of darkness, the unit completely encircled the Village usually around three o'clock. At first light, the unit moved into the Village from all sides, looking for the enemy. Latoure and the Scouts' responsibility were to act as interpreters plus tag all the enemy equipment. Attached to the unit were medical personnel who treated any and all of the sick.

Because Latoure was the ranking intelligence person with this particular Civil Action, he was invited to the Village Chief's hut. Of course, Can was at his side when the entered. Latoure treated the Chief with respect, knowing that would glean the most information. With Can's help translating Latoure's questions, much was being learned about VC activity in the area. Latoure assured the Chief that the Marines would do their part in helping the Village. While they talked, the Chief's wife prepared some food for the guests. Latoure wasn't too sure about what it was or if he should even eat it. Not wanting to insult the Chief's hospitality, he ate all that was on the plate. Almost immediately, the Chief's wife replaced the plate with another, which Latoure also ate. For the third time, the wife replaced the plate with more food.

Can leaned in and whispered, "You must leave something on the plate to show you are full and pleased with the food."

Now Latoure felt really bad, thinking he had eaten the family's weeks' worth of food. Around 1800 that evening, the civil action operation concluded, with the Marine units withdrawing.

That evening under the cover a darkness, the Viet Cong moved into the Village. First, they beat the Village Chief then raped his wife in front of him and finally beheaded him, placing his head upon a spike, leading into the Village. When Latoure heard this, his blood began to boil. He told Major Ramsey about the Chief and his wife; to which, the Major replied, "I have a plan, Sergeant Latoure. I hope it is fruitful."

Major Ramsey was a very savvy Marine, especially when it came to enemy operations. He devised an immediate action operation to catch the enemy off guard. It was quite simple actually; an Army Loach Helicopter flew around at treetop level, goading the VC into firing at the small helo. When that happened, a Marine Company-sized unit was already embarked in Hueys, either flying somewhere out of sight or on a secure landing zone, waiting to pounce on the unsuspecting enemy. It was called King Fisher.

The Major waited for three full days, wanting the VCs to get comfortable with their surrounds before ordering King Fisher to patrol the area surrounding the Village where the Chief was killed. Just as the Major had thought, the VCs couldn't resist opening fire on the small Helo. Almost immediately, the Company-sized unit landed to the south of where the helo received fire and pushed northward. The Vietcongs took off at a full run, trying to distance themselves from the Marine Corps. Once they hit the open field north of the Village, another surprise awaited them.

Because of the close proximity of the Village to Hill 55, the Major and Latoure had a ringside seat to the action from their perch on top of the Command Bunker. Once the VCs broke out into the open, a pair of Cobra gunships were waiting for them. You could clearly see the 40 mm grenades exploding among the VCs, as well as machine gun fire. The Marine Company broke through the tree line shortly after the VCs. Sergeant Latoure got to the LZ for immediate interrogation ASAP. Latoure thanked the Major for that morning's entertainment and took off running for the landing zone atop Hill 55.

Latoure knew what information was required; he had done it numerous times during Operation Pipestone Canyon while interrogating prisoners. Who, what, why, where, and how were to be asked. Can, as usual, was waiting at the LZ for Latoure and waiting for the helos to drop off the VC prisoners. The Corpsmen knelt by Latoure, also waiting; they were told wounded VCs were among the prisoners. Headquarters and Service personnel were also there to assist in any way that was required.

The first CH-46 landed, and the headquarters Marines went up the ramp and began to off-load the enemy prisoners who were on stretchers. Snowball was a self-proclaimed hero from the night the First Marines moved to Hill 55. A truck driver by MOS and a huge Marine with a round face were carrying the front of the litter. As they set down the stretcher in front of Latoure and the Corpsman, Snowball kicked the prisoner on the head on purpose. Seeing red,

Latoure jumped up and in true form, gave Snowball a horizontal butt stroke, knocking him to the ground.

"How am I supposed to get information from someone you kicked in the head? Furthermore, how would you feel if your positions were exchanged?" To say Latoure was livid would have been an understatement.

While Latoure was counseling Snowball, the Corpsman were working on the prisoner, trying to save his life.

Doc looked up at Latoure and said, "I can't find a vein!" He was almost apologetic.

Can and Latoure knelt on either side of the prisoner. Latoure knew exactly who he was. While watching the action with the Major, he saw a 40 mm grenade explode between a VC's legs, and judging by the wounds, this was that one. Latoure started by asking what they could do for the prisoner with Can translating; the VC looked at Latoure and asked for "Nuoc," which means *water*; no translation was necessary. He took his canteen and asked Doc if it was okay to give to the VC. Doc nodded yes.

After drinking the Vietcong identified himself as a Warrant Officer in the Q-Ninety-Second Battalion and answered all the tactical question he knew that Latoure and Can were going to ask without any prompting. Within two minutes of volunteering the information, his eyes rolled back in his head, passing right in front of Latoure and Can. Now with information on which unit was involved, Can and Latoure could use it to their advantage when interrogating other prisoners. At the same time, the corpsman categorized the prisoners from walking wound to those needing hospital care.

At the time, Latoure didn't know both he and Can had a shadow following them as they moved from prisoner to prisoner. After all had been interrogated by all available Intelligence and Counter Intelligence personnel for immediate Intel, the prisoners were then loaded onto trucks or those needing hospital care, helos were standing by to transport them where the prisoners would face further interrogation by those whose profession was interrogation at the POW compound. After the chopper departed, he and Can turned to leave the LZ, turning right into the face of Colonel Wilkerson, the Regimental Commander.

"I won't forget what I just saw you two accomplish, when those attempting to do the same came up empty. Outstanding job to both of you. What are your names?"

"Sergeant Latoure, sir, and this is Can, the number one Kit Carson Scout."

"I won't forget you two. That's for sure. Carry on," the Colonel said.

Latoure looked at Can and asked, "Hungry?"

Can nodded and off to the Scouts' Hut they went. Latoure had been given some B-rats during his visit at his buddy, the cook; now was a good time to break them out.

All the Scouts feasted on the dehydrated hamburgers that evening; with a little help from the beer that was left, they had themselves a party despite the 175 mm cannons firing on the other side of the berm. Luckily, Latoure didn't have to stand Midwatch that evening and fell asleep on his air mattress, totally oblivious to the artillery fire not more than two hundred meters away.

He was shaken awake by someone he did not know and heard, "The CO wants to see you ASAP."

"Let me shave and get squared away. I will be there in less than ten."

The visitor told him, "Hurry up. It's important."

Latoure got himself as squared away as he could, given the limited time he had. Luckily, Mama-san had polished his extra pair of jungle boots and pressed a set of utilities.

Latoure entered the COC, but the Colonel wasn't there. A Lieutenant asked if he was Latoure, which Latoure acknowledged. "Go to the conference center. The CO is there, Sergeant."

"Aye, aye, Sir," Latoure said as he headed out of the Command Bunker. *Where the hell is the Conference Center?* he thought to himself, thinking stopping by the S-2 would be his best bet. Luckily, he saw the Regimental Intelligence Officer heading his way.

"Follow me!" was all that was said.

They entered a hut that looked exactly like the other hundreds on Hill 55. This one, though, was open completely, and you could see the total length of the hut, fore and aft plus side to side. In the middle was a gigantic table with chairs all around it. Sitting next to the Regimental Commander was an old acquaintance—Tim Hardy, the Spook that Latoure had given a ride from Hoi An a couple months back. Latoure reached across the table and shook Hardy's hand.

The CO asked, "So you two know each other then. That's great."

"I was his taxi driver a few months back, sir."

Hardy laughed and said, "There was more to it than that, I recall."

"Let's get down to it then," the CO said.

For the next three hours, with a map of the Regiment's TAOR outlined, it was discussed how best to utilize the new sensor equipment, who was to install it, and who was to monitor it once it was in the ground. The different types of sensor equipment were explained to all present by Hardy. Latoure thought all this was way out of his league until Hardy said, "Sergeant Latoure has been vetted by the company and as of now holds a Special Intelligence, Top Secret Clearance."

That statement almost knocked Latoure out of his seat and who the hell was "the company?"

"Looks like you are it, Sergeant Latoure. You and you alone are going to be briefed on the operation of the different sensors we are going to deploy around the TAOR," The Regimental Commander said then asked the Intel Officer, "Can you afford to lose him?"

"Yes, sir, he was an added bonus from Division G-2. So no issues, sir." The two were talking like he wasn't in the room. "I need to add, Sergeant Latoure. Although you will be taking your Scouts with you as you deploy all this equipment, you are not cleared to tell them anything about their operation. Understood?"

"Aye, aye, Sir," Latoure replied.

"As a reward, you get to take a three-day trip to Saigon this coming week," the CO told him then added, "Everyone out except Hardy, Latoure, and me."

It was a blur of assholes and elbows as all in the conference room hurried out. When all had departed, the CO said, "Okay, Mr. Hardy, tell us about your equipment and their function."

During the next two hours, each individual piece was covered with each having their own code, which was transmitted to a radio that looked like a PRC-77; although this had a small window which displayed a number relating to that piece of sensor equipment. The last part of the puzzle was Latoure's trip to Saigon, where he was to attend SLAR School, short for side-looking airborne radar. It was a lot of information; however, Latoure felt he understood over 90 percent of what was explained.

"I will leave you and Mr. Hardy to go over the final details. Thank you, Mr. Hardy." The CO nodded at Latoure, who had risen and was standing at the position of attention while the CO departed the conference center.

Operational details like how far each sensor would transmit, how long they would operate on their internal batteries, which piece augmented another, and a basic understanding of what and where Hardy would put what piece around Hill 55. Before Latoure realized it, another two hours had passed; his mind was filled with both tactical and operational information on the sensors and their deployment.

The smaller pieces of equipment were to be stored in a footlocker at the Regimental S-2. The Regimental Intelligence Officer and Latoure had the only access to it plus an underground bunker a few meters from the Regimental S-2, which provided security for the larger pieces of equipment. During Latoure's assignment at the Third Battalion, a new regimental intelligence officer had been assigned. Captain Smyth was a career 0202, the MOS for a career intelligence officer. Latoure already respected Captain Smyth, especially after he told Latoure that the sensor deployment was Latoure's responsibility, and he would not get involved except for giving assistance when requested.

It didn't make any sense to Latoure not being allowed to take any weapon with him on the flight to Saigon to attend the SLAR training. Luckily for him, one of the Scouts had a folding fishing knife that when opened became a formable weapon. He only took a ditty bag filled with his shaving kit and a change of underwear; he was told to wear civilian clothes. "No visible rank." The bag was in the seat next to him on the KC-130 military aircraft. Which added to the confusion on why he couldn't bring at least his .45. It felt like he just closed his eyes when the aircraft began its landing at Saigon. With no one stopping him or asking for identification, he exited the terminal. Almost directly in front of him was a Vietnamese holding a handwritten sign with Latoure's name on it.

"I'm Latoure," he told the local, who didn't answer but attempted to take the ditty bag from him. That wasn't going to happen even when the local gave Latoure a look of anger. Trust is a funny thing, and Latoure immediately did not trust this local.

Latoure followed the Vietnamese to an olive drab military sedan. Latoure opened the rear door and took a seat. Quickly, they were on their way to places unknown. The driver was making so many turns both left and right and even headed back toward the airport twice. The hair of Sergeant Latoure's neck began to bristle, so quietly, he unzipped the ditty bag and extended the blade of the fishing knife. The sun had already begun to set while the local continued making crazy turns. Visions of being taken to a Vietcong stronghold went through his head. If he made one more turn down another dark street, Latoure was going to put a stop to it with force if necessary. Halfway down the street, the vehicle stopped in front of a huge iron gate.

"You go there" was all that was said. Latoure was happy not to be inside the vehicle and now had room to move if necessary.

It was all for naught; there was a very large sign clearly reading MACV as he entered the compound. He walked up the steps and entered the building, where an Army Spec 4 sat at a desk, controlling access. Latoure handed his orders to the Spec 4, who almost immediately told him, "Marine Liaison, second door on the right."

Latoure thanked the duty and proceeded to check in. Once inside the Marine Liaison office, the only person present was a Marine Corporal. Latoure handed the Corporal his orders, who stated, "Bad news, Sergeant, the school has been canceled. How long you want to stay in Saigon before heading back up north?"

"What are you talking about?" Latoure asked.

"Most like to spend three or four days on a mini R&R when things like this happen," the liaison told him.

"I need to get back. I have beaucoup things to do and no time to do it in. Where can I sack out?"

"I wasn't expecting you, so it will take a few minutes to get you squared away, Sergeant. See that building with the lights on the porch?"

"Yeah!"

"That is the ARVN Major's house. You can get a beer there while I hook you up."

"Why the heck would I want to go there?" Latoure said.

And the Liaison replied, "Trust me."

Latoure had brought $100 MPC (Military Pay Certificates) with him just in case, so off he went to have that beer.

As he walked up the steps, someone opened the door and told him in English to please come in. The entrance led into the kitchen where there was a '50s-style table with four or five chairs around it. Latoure took the seat where he could watch both the entrance and the door leading into the kitchen. The ARVN Major's house was close to the MACV Compound but still was outside its protective walls. He was offered a beer by the older woman who was either the Major's wife or a Mama-san looking after the home. As he drank his beer, a steady stream of Vietnamese girls came into the kitchen to check him out. Most were between 6 to 8 on the beauty scale; nothing really wonderful until she entered.

She was an 11 on a scale of 1 to 10. She was biracial, half European and half Chinese. Those who have traveled the Orient sometimes were lucky enough to gaze upon these treasures. Instead of leaving the kitchen like the other girls did, this wonder sat across from him, looking deeply into his eyes.

"Buy me beer?" she asked in English with a very heavy accent. Latoure motioned to the lady of the house, who brought over two beers, one for each of them. She said something to the girl, who nodded as Mama-san left the kitchen after locking the back door. Song explained that her mother was Chinese, while her father was a French diplomat. Both were killed late in the Vietnamese–French War of the mid-1950s. She was orphaned, and this was the only place she could find work. She also explained that the Major was good to the girls; he gave them protection and a place to stay. Of course, Latoure's mind went to the fact that he used the girls as prostitutes to pad his bankroll.

She offered Latoure a place to sleep that night rather than returning to the MACV Compound. Throwing caution to the wind, he accepted her invitation but told her that he must return to the Compound first thing in the morning. She didn't ask what branch, rank, or any personal information. Latoure's French was limited to his high school education, but he tried to converse in both English and French with Song. He couldn't believe how beautiful she was; given a different path, she could have been a movie star. She grabbed his hand even before they had finished their beer and led him farther into the house. It was a well-kept home; he looked around as they made their way to a set of stairs with an old-time ornate wooden banister. They entered her room, and almost immediately, when the door closed, she kissed him passionately.

They made slow, tender love for the next hour, exploring each other's bodies from head to foot, taking turns. She asked him more than once, "You take me to America, okay?"

Of course, Latoure didn't answer her, not wanting to get her hopes up. It was around 2200 when they entered her room, but soon after, time seemed to stand still. She would not allow him to stop making love to her. Over and over, she did everything in her power to bring him back to life so they could once again make love; always with the same request, "You take me to America, okay?"

She didn't allow him to sleep at all. The sun began to shine through her curtains; for the ninth time, they began to make love. He was in pain but did his part to please her. He felt terrible as he dressed, saying he must go check in at the Compound.

"You come back, okay?" she pleaded.

"I will try, Song." He turned and walked out of her life forever.

He checked in with the Marine Liaison. There was a flight returning to Da Nang at noon, and he got his gear together, to which Latoure held up his ditty bag and said, "This is it."

"I'll get you a ride to the airport, Sergeant Latoure."

Latoure thanked the Corporal for his help both with the flight and his insistence to visit the ARVN Major's House. By 1700 that night, he was back on Hill 55 ready to begin the Electronic Barrier around the Hill.

CHAPTER 9
The Big Picture: Hill 55 Extended

The Command Staff at the Division, known as the powers that be, which were way above Latoure's pay grade, assigned the Electronic Barrier for the Division Tactical Area Of Responsibility (TAOR) to Hardy and his local nationals. Hardy had access to all the Major Sensor equipment, which covered large areas, such as the Balance Pressure Unit (BPU) which would be perfect for covering known ingress or egress routes used by both the Vietcong and by their big brothers, the North Vietnamese Army (NVA).

Latoure's responsibility was the immediate area surround Hill 55; out to a distance that would hopefully prevent anymore Lob Bomb attacks. Latoure had both PPS-6 personal radar and Personal Seismic Intrusion Devices (PSIDs). The overall plan after the installation of all the sensor equipment was to set up a monitoring station on Hill 55. Each sensor had a different numerical code, so the person assigned was to monitor the equipment utilizing the portal, which displayed the code for whatever sensor was tripped.

Hardy had already gotten busy installing the BPU around the area of Dong Den, north of Da Nang. It had been tested, and artillery was locked in on the route, ready for use when the sensor was activated. Hardy and his crew were already heading south to the area known as Arizona Territory to install a second BPU.

A semicircle was drawn on a 1:50,000 map at a distance of 1,500 meters completely encircling Hill 55. It was thought that four or five separate strings of three PSIDs each would be enough to place that barrier around the First Marines and its supporting elements on Hill 55. Not to be outdone, the artillery personnel had their own piece of electronic equipment. It was a huge box that contained a laser, which could be aimed at a target, and the target's eight-digit location would be designated almost instantaneously. Latoure was given six weeks to install all the sensors as well as monitor them whenever he was back on Hill 55.

With his five-man Scout team, Latoure set out on foot at first light to place the first string. There was a finger that stuck out to the northeast from Hill 55. It was a perfect spot for the PPS-6 to verify the readings from the sensor string the team was getting ready to place. Even though the Scouts were careful not to be observed while placing the sensor under the middle unit, Latoure placed a fragmentation grenade should the enemy try to dig it up. The small explosive device inside the sensor only destroyed the electronics, not the entire piece. Latoure radioed the artillery people who had been watching the team at work from the largest tower on Hill 55, ready to try out their new piece of equipment. Latoure cautioned the Scouts to look toward Charlie Ridge and not back at the Hill until he gave the all clear, then popped a smoke grenade close to but not on the center sensor. Within seconds the all clear was given, and the team continued around Hill 55 as if they were on a clearing mission.

That evening Latoure sat in a lawn chair on top of the COC Bunker, ready to monitor all the electronics. He had two trained PPS-6 Operators and two of his Marine Scouts on the finger, just in case the enemy went to see what the team was doing that morning. Latoure had the codes for the two BPUs Hardy installed plus the three PSIDs the team put in the ground earlier. It was only a matter of time now. The Regimental Commander and Major Ramsey climbed up on top of the COC bunker to see what Latoure had set up. Not thirty seconds after they knelt beside him, the first code flashed on the small screen.

"What was that?" The Major asked.

"Sensor 1 on string Alpha, Sir." He answered, while reaching for the field phone, giving it a crank. "Patch me through to the Scouts out on the finger."

"Corporal Kirby, we have activity on the strings. Get them to do a sweep with the PPS and let me know what they get." While Latoure waited for a reply the code for Sensor 2 flashed. "They are moving left to right, Sir."

Latoure heard Kirby say, "Positive ID on the movement."

Curiosity killed the cat, he thought to himself. "Colonel, we have movement in the area of String Alpha. Request a Fire Mission?"

"Go for it!" the Colonel replied.

Now on the radio to the Eleventh Marines, "Fire, Mission String Alpha, Battery One, over."

"Shot out!"

Three rounds impacted right on the path alongside the sensors, which codes flashed like mad. The Colonel looked at Latoure and said, "One more time."

He radioed the artillery folks and ordered up another battery one.

During the artillery, Latoure didn't hear Corporal Kirby on the landline, but now as things quieted down, he picked up the field phone and listened. "Sir, Corporal Kirby just told me he could see bodies flying through the air both times and is requesting permission to go check. Sir, it is only Corporal Kirby and a Kit Carson there with the PPS-6 operators. Too risky. We can check in the a.m.?"

"First light you take your Scouts and check it out, Sergeant Latoure. Well done to all." The Colonel and the Major climbed down from the top of the COC. A check that next morning revealed two broken AK-47s and numerous blood trails heading away from Hill 55. None of the sensors were damaged by the artillery; in fact the rounds proved even more, covering them with flying dirt.

The previous night's demonstration sold the usefulness of Sensors to both the Commander and Major Ramsey. String Bravo would be installed the following week. It was felt that too much movement around the Hill would attract too much attention. The sensors around Hill 55 were going to be installed; two strings around six thousand meters apart, approximately four thousand to five thousand meters away with the second two strings placed on either end of Hill 55. The thought was the two strings farthest from the hill would give ample warning of approaching enemy. The closest would be used to bring artillery fire down on the enemy. Although Dodge City was leveled during Pipestone Canyon, it was felt that one or two strings would give the Marines a heads-up if any enemy approached from that direction.

Sergeant Latoure and his Scouts installed the four different strings to the west of Hill 55 over the next month. Along with the BPUs that Hardy's team placed, monitoring the equipment, seldom was there a boring duty. Late February, they began the drawdown of additional units throughout Vietnam. Staff Sergeant Stone, Latoure's friend and bridge partner, had rotated back to the "World," as it was called. The new Administration Chief wasn't as pleasant as Stone was; in fact, he was rubbing many of the Marines who had been in-country for almost a year, if not longer, had just about enough of him. So when a runner came to the top of the Command Bunker telling Latoure to report to the Admin Chief as soon as possible (ASAP), Latoure stowed away all the monitoring equipment then headed for the Regimental Administration, hoping to put out whatever fire the new Admin Chief was fanning.

"Pack your gear. You are rotating out in the morning aboard a troop carrier returning to the States. You have up to thirty days' leave to use if you so desire." Surprised, Latoure asked where he was to be assigned. "Second Marine Aircraft Wing, Cherry Point, North Carolina," the Staff Sergeant told Latoure.

"There must be some mistake. I still have thirty days left on my tour, and I also am in the middle of an assignment," Latoure told the S-1 Chief as much as he could, not knowing his clearance or access level.

"I don't care if you have a personal letter from the Commandant of the Marine Corps. You are leaving by ship in the morning from Red Beach. Here are your Official Orders. A six-by-six is leaving at 0600."

He felt there was no use in getting into a pissing contest with the Admin Chief, so he picked up his orders and went to pack what little gear he had.

On his way to his Hooch, he swung by the Command Center. The Commander nor Major Thirey were inside. The Duty Officer asked if he could help, so Latoure tore off the last copy of his orders, requesting the Duty Officer either give it to the CO or Major Ramsey when they returned.

"Can do, Sergeant Latoure, but it will be late tonight before they return. Division is having some big planning session, and they will be returning by Helo tonight." Latoure thanked the Duty Officer and headed down the hill to pack his gear.

When he got to the Hooch, all the Scouts who had been with him from the beginning were packing their gear as well. Only a newly assigned Lance Corporal plus Can and Tang were to remain. After all their gear was packed and ready, it was time to deplete the booze and beer they had remaining. Latoure had a glass of bourbon but no beer; the Black Label gave him a major headache when he drank it. The evening was spent telling war stories about what they all had experienced during their tour. Lance Corporal Winters's eyes kept getting larger and larger as the stories became bolder. Can and Tang joined the Scouts, promising to take care of the new guy.

Around 0530, they all grabbed their gear and headed toward the staging area where the six-by-six trucks waited for them. It surprised Latoure that there were four trucks, which meant almost one hundred Marines or Corpsmen were leaving Hill 55. As always, the trucks were loaded by rank. Latoure attempted to ride with the Scouts, but that was not to be. The sun was just rising over the South China Sea as the trucks departed Hill 55. A lone jeep was following the convoy very closely; the passenger was waving his hand, trying to signal the drivers to no avail. When the convoy passed through the gate at Red Beach, Latoure noticed the guards saluting the passenger in the jeep and pointing toward the dock where the trucks were headed. Some form of military decorum was attempted as the Marines jumped from the trucks. The jeep driver pulled up very close to the formation. He heard his name being yelled over and over, "Sergeant Latoure, Sergeant Latoure."

Latoure grabbed his gear and moved toward the voices. It was the Regimental Commander and his personal driver. "Sergeant

Latoure, there must be some mistake. You still have the Sensors to install in and around Dodge City," the Colonel told Latoure.

"I tried to tell the Admin Chief, but he refused to listen, sir."

"I will have a conversation with him when we return."

"Sir, I don't want to be charged with missing movement for not boarding the ship."

"Come with me, Sergeant."

"Aye, aye, sir."

Assholes and elbows were flying all over the dock as the First Marine Regiment Commanding Officer strolled toward the ship and the Duty Officer. As they approached, the CO told Latoure to give him a copy of his orders, which, of course, he did. Then He placed the copy in the Duty Officer's hand, telling him that Sergeant Latoure would not be boarding, and any questions should be directed to him personally. A pen strike was all it took as Latoure's name was stricken from the boarding roster.

Every eye was on the Colonel and some Sergeant walking in-step and abreast of the Regimental Commander. Once in the jeep, the CO turned to Latoure and told him, "That ship has an eleven- to fourteen-day sailing time to the West Coast. I will guarantee you will be in California long before that ship docks, Sergeant. Just put in that last string in Dodge City, and you will be on your way."

"Aye, aye, Sir!" Latoure replied. Once back on Hill 55, the CO told Latoure to give him his orders so they can be modified for a flight to the States.

"Lance Corporal Winters, get over here." Winters looked surprised that Sergeant Latoure was back. "Sit down on the footlocker, Winters." For the next two hours, Latoure explained within reason the operation of the PSIDs. Winters was already familiar with the PPS-6, having manned that position a few times. "You are the only one beside the CO and Major Ramsey who knows about the sensors. Tomorrow, we are going to Dodge City and install one or two sensor strings."

"No problem, Sergeant Latoure. I've got a handle on it."

Latoure headed back up the hill to the COC to check with Major Ramsey if he was available. Fortunately, the Major was at his desk; he looked up, smiled and asked Latoure what he needed.

"What unit or units are operating in or around Dodge City?" was Latoure's question.

Major Ramsey checked and discovered there was a Platoon from the First Battalion Alpha Company assigned to set up a Platoon Patrol Base the day after tomorrow.

"Sir, I need permission to go out with them," Latoure asked.

"Shouldn't be an issue. The Colonel already told me what was going on," the Major answered. "I will check back tomorrow to see which Platoon and who I should check in with. Only Lance Corporal Winters is left. I will bring him up to speed on what we are trying to do."

"I knew you would have a handle on it, Sergeant Latoure."

Latoure grabbed a map off the Intel Duty Desk and went to the S-2. He gave Lance Corporal Winters an Interim Secret Clearance, signed off by the Regimental Intel Officer, then went to the S-1 to place the clearance in Winter's Service Record Book. Before heading down to the Scouts' Hooch, Latoure explained to Winters that he now had a Secret Clearance with Limited Access to information pertaining to the Sensor operations in and around Hill 55. As he drew the sensor strings and the codes for each on the map, he made certain that no one had access to this map, and the sooner he could memorize it, the better. He also told Winters about Mr. Hardy, just in case he should show up on the hill unannounced. Finally, he told Winters they would be going into the field in two days; at first, teasingly, he said, "Just you and I, Marine, against all the VCs in Dodge City."

Winters's eyes bugged out of his head until he told him that they would be protecting a Platoon from Alpha Company as well.

"Study up. Get some rest. You will need it."

Monitoring the sensors that evening was really boring. There was no movement anywhere as he and Winters monitored the Portal until just about first light, and the codes from the BPU northeast of the hill began to flash. "Are we going to call arty on them?" Winters asked.

"No, the BPUs just let us know they are moving into the area. Our strings are the ones we call arty in on. I am not sure who will do the monitoring once I leave here, but it will be up to you to show them the ropes."

They had one more night of monitoring the strings, which they stopped around 0300 so they could get ready to meet up with the Platoon from Alpha. Sergeant Latoure checked in with the Platoon Commander, who had already spent six months in-country, which was a plus. As they moved off Hill 55, heading for Dodge City, Latoure began to notice familiar things from when he visited Dodge City during Pipestone Canyon. When the Platoon reached their assigned area, Latoure and Winters kept moving farther south, approximately one thousand meters away, known as a click. Latoure looked for signs taught to him by Can, which told VCs which way was safe and which wasn't. Latoure noticed a break in the elephant grass, which already had grown to over six feet despite being leveled less than a few months prior.

Latoure buried the first sensor with Winters, observing then moving two hundred meters farther, letting Winters bury and arm the second and in another two hundred meters, the third in the sensor string. It was only a little before noon, so the two of them moved farther east along the edge of the elephant grass, being wary of booby traps or punji pits. They came upon a large clearing with a firepit. Looking for an ingress or egress route, they found what they were seeking. This time Latoure allowed Winters to place all three of the sensors and arm them. With information recorded, they began retracing their steps back to the Platoon Patrol Base.

When they got to within one thousand meters off to the left, both heard definite movement. Latoure called the Lieutenant on the radio very quietly, asking if he had sent out the nightly patrol as of yet. Miffed, the Lieutenant replied, "Of course not. I know what I am doing."

"Well then, you know about the VCs who are about one thousand meters at your three o'clock then, Lieutenant?"

"What did you just say?" the Lieutenant asked.

Latoure told him again but added that he and Latoure were going to check it out and to please standby. With a definite change of heart, the Lieutenant answered in the affirmative. What the two of them stumbled upon was four VCs setting up a bamboo, aiming stakes, then two additional bamboo poles which cradled two separate 122 mm rockets aimed at Da Nang. He radioed the Lieutenant and informed him what was happening. They had two choices. Winters and Latoure could open fire, hopefully killing or wounding all four, or use the 60 mm mortar the Lieutenant had. They could drop some rounds on it. The negative was in firing the mortar; the Platoon's position would be compromised.

A thought came to Winters, who told Latoure, "Why not act as a blocking force and have the Lieutenant send out a patrol to contact the enemy. That way the position wouldn't be compromised."

Latoure radioed Winters's idea, which the Lieutenant agreed. Latoure and Winters moved to either side of the trail, aiming at the area where they thought the VC would be running from. A radio call from the Lieutenant informed them the patrol was silently moving to catch the VCs with their pants down. Twenty minutes later, all hell broke loose as the patrol opened fire. One VC thought he had escaped but ran almost over Winters, who tackled the VC then disarmed him. With his wrist bound, the two of them joined the Patrol who were all smiles. No Marine was hit, and the rockets were captured intact. By the time the contact was over and all had returned to the Platoon Patrol Base, it was so dark you couldn't see the hand in front of your face. The Lieutenant was extremely pleased with that day's activity and was thankful to Latoure for the solution he came up with. Latoure told the Lieutenant that it was Lance Corporal Winters's idea, and the credit should go to him. The Lieutenant slapped both on the backs and told them to take the rest of the night off; they would call them if they needed them.

The Intel Types made a U shape out of some sandbags that weren't being used, providing enough cover should the VCs come visiting later that night. The Platoon had taken charge of the POW, but Latoure and Winters would be taking him with them in the morning when they returned to Hill 55. Winters set up the Portal like a kid with a new present; he began to monitor it.

Latoure was thinking maybe they should move the second sensor string farther west of the clearing. He mentioned it to Winters, who said that he could bring out another set of sensors and deploy them now, knowing the main VC routes.

As Latoure lay down, he was beseeched by what seemed like a million mosquitoes. Rolling down his sleeves did little to stop the stings. By now Winters had been swarmed by the insects. They created a makeshift roof of empty sandbags as well as a curtain and lay down. The rest of the evening, they took turns smoking and trying to keep the bugs off their faces. The next morning, Latoure had over a hundred bites on his stomach, while Winters had almost the same amount. He had a cool water scrub and packed up their gear.

They went to get the VC. He had a couple of bruises on his face, which Latoure let slide, not wanting to get into a pissing match with the Marines of Alpha.

Latoure had the VC walk point, with his .45 drawn to discourage the VC from trying anything stupid. They made excellent time returning to Hill 55, where they dropped the prisoner off at the Interrogator/Translator's Hooch. He told Winters to stow the sensor equipment, and he would catch up with him at the Scouts' Hut.

He went into the command bunker and was pleased to find both the CO and Major Ramsey waiting. He debriefed the patrol's actions and mentioned how outstanding a Marine Winters was becoming. He also told them of the need for an additional sensor string around Dodge City, and Lance Corporal Winters was well aware of where it should be placed. Then much to Latoure's surprise, both the CO and the Major shook his hand and thanked him for doing such an outstanding job. Then the CO told him to go to the Regimental S-1 and see the new Sergeant that was the Acting Admin Chief. With a heavy heart, he did a military about-face and left the Bunker for the last time.

The Admin Chief came from the Division; the whereabouts of the Staff Sergeant was unknown to everyone in the S-1. The only change to his orders was that he now would be flying back in the Flying Tiger Freedom Bird, leaving Da Nang around noon the following day. The aircrew would be spending the night on Okinawa for what was called Crew Rest and flying back to Travis Airforce Base the day after. It looked like the CO kept his word, and Latoure would be in the States a full three days before the ship.

CHAPTER 10
The Freedom Bird:
Club Misty

The aircraft felt like a sauna after thirteen months of moving freely through the jungles of Vietnam. It was also filled with anticipation almost to the man of having done one's duty to God and Country. The aircraft doors were closed, and that action only added to the personnel discomfort inside the plane. Finally, after what seemed like an eternity, the overhead fans began to circulate warm air throughout the cabin. Everyone aboard felt the tractor push the Flying Tiger aircraft back from its position at the terminal, and then the engine increased power, heading for the takeoff position.

They were at zero to twenty thousand feet in a heartbeat; the right wing was lowered as the plane turned toward Okinawa, its designated crew rest assignment. Kadena Air Force Base and the island of Okinawa was a little more than two hours away. The military on board seemed to be holding their breath until the captain came over the speakers and announced, "Gentlemen, you have departed the airspace of the Republic of Vietnam."

Hearing those words could have been translated to "Let the party get started" because that was exactly the mood of all aboard. *Okinawa, here I come,* Latoure thought to himself.

By the time all aboard had been processed and assigned transportation to their temporary housing by Military Branch, the Marines who were to be housed at Camp Foster boarded those familiar gray buses for that short trip down Highway 58. Latoure knew where the Transit NCO Barracks were located, having spent ten days waiting for Corporal Jones to change his orders and broke from the ranks after listening to what time they were to muster for the trip back to Kadena Air Force Base in the morning. It was too late in the day to try and catch up with Corporal Jones at work, so Latoure opted for the three *S*'s after laying out his civilian clothes on his rack. As he was getting ready, Mama-san passed by his door, and bless her heart, she remembered Latoure as she quickly picked up his clothes to press for him as he showered. She had a smile from ear to ear. *Maybe she really did like him,* he thought, moving toward the head.

Thirty minutes later, he was all dressed and ready for evening chow. He stopped by the permanent personnel NCO Quarters, hoping to find Corporal Jones there. Of course, he wasn't; but Corporal Denny, the Supply NCO that took care of him, was. Denny told him Corporal Jones had married Midori plus got his orders changed to a three-year accompanied tour. He asked Denny if he was going to chow, which Denny acknowledge, so the two of them headed up the hill toward mess hall.

"I have to stop by the PX first, Corporal Denny, and get some smokes for Mama-san in the NCO transit barracks," Latoure said.

"No problem, Sarge," Denny replied.

The food at the mess hall was miles above what he had been existing on in Vietnam; between baloney sandwiches on midwatch, C rations in the field, and green eggs at the Hill 55 chow hall.

"I am going to go to the NCO Club after I give Mama-san these smokes. Want to have a drink with me, Corporal Denny?"

"I would like to, Sergeant, but we have a field day tonight for all personnel," Denny answered.

"Been there, done that!" Latoure said. "Thanks for the company, Corporal Denny. Hope to meet you somewhere, sometime."

"Oohrah!" they answered in unison.

Mama-san had his room squared away, thinking that he was going to be on Okinawa for a while. He caught up with her, gave her the carton of Marlboros, and thanked her once again.

He had a bourbon and Coke, plus twenty dollars in the slot machines at an almost deserted NCO Club. Latoure hoped it wasn't too early to venture into the Village of Kitamae. Recalling where Corporal Jones and Midori's apartment was located, he walked there with some pep in his step. He really was looking forward to seeing all three of his friends, especially Michiko. The door was answered by Midori, who stared at Latoure with the deer-in-the-headlight look.

Corporal Jones called from inside, "Who is it?" Michiko was tongue-tied. "Ca-chan, who is there?" Still no reply.

So Latoure answered for her, "Get off your fat ass and come see who is at your door, Marine."

Jones did just that. He had been promoted to Sergeant, which was well deserved, in Latoure's mind. After a handshake, hug, and slap on the back, Latoure was invited in.

Jones was filled with questions about Latoure's time in Vietnam. Latoure gave the mini version before moving the conversation to what he really wanted to know. Latoure's feelings sank when he first learned that Michiko had married an air force airman and returned to the US together. The dagger that pierced his heart was Michiko gave birth to a healthy baby boy in December of last year. Latoure could do the math; more than likely, the child was his.

"Why didn't you write me and let me know?"

"She wouldn't allow it. You know how these Okinawan women are, buddy."

Midori handed Latoure a dozen pictures of the baby; his baby, no doubt about it. "What is his name?" Latoure asked.

"Does it make a difference, pal?" Jones asked.

"It does to me."

Midori reached across and turned the last photo over; printed on the back was "Larry Sutter, born December 25, 1969."

Suddenly, he no longer felt like going to Club Misty, but Midori still worked there and insisted on Latoure returning to finish off the bottle of Seagram's he had purchased a year ago.

He was glad that Midori insisted on going to the Club Misty rather than crying with his beer alone in the Transit NCO Quarters. Sometime during the night, Latoure asked Midori and Jones to let Michiko know that he came back for her please. If they did or didn't do it, he would never know, for life went on.

Latoure's tour of duty with the Second Marine Aircraft Wing was short-lived. He had a six-month tour of the Mediterranean, flying in the General's T-8 jet both ways, and a few color details the Marine Corps sent him orders to, where he felt he belonged. He was at the Third Marine Regiment stationed at Kaneohe Bay, Hawaii. From there, Latoure attended intelligence schools both on the island and the Naval School located at San Diego, California. The school that surprised him most was the army school located at Fort Huachuca, Arizona. It was an Unattended Ground Sensor School. Of all the Instructors and students, Latoure was the only one with practical experience deploying sensors. So often, the instructors deferred to him when talking deployment.

When he returned to the Third Marines, two new Scouts fresh out of Vietnam had been assigned to the intelligence Scouts. One of the two, he vaguely remembered because he was in the sensor installation mode at the time. This Marine told him about Can and Tang. First, Tang saved a lance corporal from drowning when they were trying to cross the river back onto Ga Noi Island for a new operations. Tang received the Navy or Marine Corps Lifesaving Medal.

"You probably don't want to hear what happened to Can, Sergeant Latoure."

"Why is that?"

"First, I want to say that I would have gone to war with Can anytime or anyplace. That being said, he was killed when he dove on top of a Marine that was walking point, who tripped a 105 mm daisy chain booby trap. The Marine escaped with minor wounds. Can was killed outright. He was awarded the Bronze Star with Combat V for valor." Latoure let the information sink in then shook the Scout's hand, thanking him for bringing him up to speed.

He had already made his mind up that he would dedicate his life from that point forward to GOD, COUNTRY, and CORPS. Semper Fidelis, Marines.

ABOUT THE AUTHOR

 L. R. LaVancher is a Retired US Marine Master Gunnery Sergeant with twenty-five years of service. He was at a myriad of duty stations from Parris Island to retiring at Marine Barracks, Washington, DC. His Military occupational specialties included Aviation Ordnance upon entering, changing to Military intelligence, and finally retiring as a morale administrative director. He had additional assignments as drill instructor and instructor-inspector at NAS Atlanta and NAS South Weymouth. He went in combat with the First Marines and units of that regiment in the Vietnam Conflict, on which this novel is based. He is an award-winning artist, using both graphite and watercolors, which he now spends his time. He is currently writing *A Return to Oki*, six years hence from Vietnam.

CPSIA information can be obtained
at www.ICGtesting.com
Printed in the USA
BVHW032242010721
611020BV00001B/17

9 781646 541799